THE BROKEN BONES BOOK OF HORROR

by

Tony Hazel

Two Kittens Publishing - 2025

For Sarah.
Without you, I would
be nothing.

Two Kittens Publishing
The Whitehouse, West Street, Sompting BN15 0AP
admin@twokittenspublishing.co.uk

Paperback Edition 2024

Contents

Preface

What follows are the short stories I wrote for the 'Broken Bones Horror Theatre', podcast. 'A Love in the Mist', the first episode debuted on 29th December 2023.

The stories were all written whilst holding down an awful job, I hated. I wrote after work and whenever I could find some time. Likewise, there were many late nights recording, directing and producing the tales. I also produced short promotional videos for the entire second season, which I can barely believe I found the time to do.

The stories are read by a variety of voices, some real people, some inappropriately repurposed AI. The AI voices could be seen as being a little controversial, however I think the fact that 'Thomas the AI Ghoul', who reads 'A Love in the Mist' was originally conceived as an AI mediation bot, actually adds to the other-worldliness of the reading.

I was lucky enough to be able to have some well known people read some of the stories. The late Saul Reichlin (prolific audiobook vocal artist and actor) was the first, followed by Alex Lowe, (Phoenix Nights, Clinton Baptiste), Eva Pope (Coronation Street, Waterloo Road) and BC Camplight ('Song Behemoth'). Friends and family provided the remaining voices.

There follows a list of all the readers who have contributed to the podcast;

Season 1

A Love in the Mist	Thomas the AI Ghoul
Three Steps Behind	Saul Reichlin

The Capsule	Nicole the AI Psychopath
37 Lombard Street	Tony Hazel
Friends Reunited	Sarah Powell
Nightmare	Tony Hazel

Season 2

Mill Hill	Alex Lowe
The Hexham Heads Pts I & II	Eva Pope
Stone Tape Theory	BC Camplight
Via Dolorosa	Nicholas Stellmacher
Four Minutes	Tony Hazel

Many thanks to all of them for their contribution. It really helped me complete the series and gave it some heft.

If you'd like to read along, the podcast can be found here:

https://tinyurl.com/4h4hs22u

Forward

by Sarah Powell

There comes, I am sure, a time in everyone's life, when you look at your husband, wife, partner or flat mate and wonder who on earth you are living with. The question, which had been niggling away at me for some time, rushed to the fore with surprising alacrity whilst watching Tony, somewhat hamfistedly, painting some of the ceiling of our downstairs hall. 'Chasing shadows,' he said, in between the cries, moans and groans of the 'older decorator'.

It's impossible to read about people boring into their own skulls with a cordless drill, or eating their dates, not the ones with a stone, without, at the very least, wondering what kind of mind produced these thoughts, that became ideas, that became podcasts and eventually found their way into print. People have mused for centuries on the loose line between fiction and reality; in the wee small hours, lying in bed with this mind, the one that also used my mother and I as models for another desolate tale, that ended with, not only my death, but my eternal damnation, one can't help but notice how this question comes sharply into focus. Should I run now, and take the not so subtle hint, or just put it down to artistic licence?

There's no doubt about it, anyone who lives with an 'artist', will be used to the cycle of confidence, arrogance, then immediate self doubt, that constitutes the general self obsession you've learnt to navigate on a daily basis. The irony is, Tony's writing career started, as a way of encouraging me to write again. It worked, initially, we wrote Princess Porcelaina together, a romp of a story, not a daemon in sight, then I fell back into my full-on job, and Tony quietly, but often noisily, started writing Three Steps Behind, for a BBC Christmas ghost story competition. He didn't win, he didn't get his story broadcast; I thought he should have: it's an atmospheric seasonal spine chiller, the perfect accompaniment to your pickles and cheese for Christmas Eve.

After the initial self loathing and suicidal tendencies had passed, he carried on writing and saving, engaging actually quite famous actors and his favourite singer, to read his new stories. After a day of IT phone support, he'd be tapping away upstairs in the dark, headphones on, vetting an array of unsettling noises, which would later become podcast soundtracks, whilst I'd get home from work, wondering where my dinner was. He refused to talk about any of the stories until they were finished, and, in spite of my creative writing MA and English teaching career, refused to take any advice, or just one tiny, but important, bit at the end of Hexham Heads. I was, however, 'allowed' to edit them all though, a pretty annoying job, to be fair; dyslexia is one thing, but stubbornness, bloody mindedness and total refusal to learn the basics of direct speech punctuation, any use of commas or capital letters whatsoever, or even the vague notion of what constitutes a sentence, just means I'm destined to keep correcting the same mistakes until the end of time. Still, he paints a mean picture, mean enough to have passed his own MA in fine art.

The Broken Bones Book of Horror is like Hieronymus Bosch meets William Blake and Alice Cooper and they all get shafted up the Tower of Babel; a compelling compilation, or rare access to the aphotic ramblings of a nascent serial killer? Read it and make your own mind up, then be happy if you live with a man, or woman, who works in an office and likes a kebab on a Friday night.

A Love In The Mist

Tracy looked lovingly at Steve as she ran his bath, it was just about up to his chest now as he lay back in the warming water. She put a hand in to test the temperature. It was hot but could have been hotter, so she turned the dial up a little and let some of the water out. Hotter water soon took it's place and the bath continued to fill.

"How is that my darling?" She looked into Steve's eyes and stroked his brow. Steve shook his head and shot her a look.

"Not hot enough? Oh dear, I'll turn it up a bit".

Steve exhaled and his chest fell below the water line.

Tracy checked the dial again and turned it up a little further.

"There" she said "that should do it, I don't want to scald you. I'll go and make some tea."

Tracy hadn't had much luck with love. There had been boyfriends and the occasional girlfriend of course, but none of them stuck around for very long. She would go on dates, 2nd dates, and sometimes even a weekend away, but soon enough they would stop responding and she'd have to start all over again.

Entering the kitchen, she flicked the kettle on, and ran a finger along the worktop. This time she thought it would be different. She had met Steve through a dating app, 'Finders Keepers'. It claimed to be different from other apps in that it was only for those people looking for long term love and commitment. This was Tracy down to a tee.

She yearned for romantic love. Love that would only grow and blossom in time. She read a lot of romance novels and she loved the idea of being in love and being loved.

The kettle came to a rolling boil, and she poured the scalding water over a tea bag, freshly plucked from the caddy, into an oversized mug.

When Steve picked her out on the app, she was a little unsure as to whether he would make a good match. He lived alone and, by his own admission, he hadn't had a lot of success or experience with women. He was quite shy, and not especially good looking. Working in an insurance company wasn't the most glamorous of jobs. He worked from home a lot, so didn't see that many people unless he really made an effort to do so.

Occasionally, he would, of an evening, go to his local pub, buy a pint of ale, and sit in the corner, on his own and read a book or look at his phone to pass the time. Sometimes, one of the barmaids would feel sorry for him and stop and chat while they were clearing adjacent tables.

On one of these occasions, as it was quiet, one of the barmaids, Lucy, had sat down next to him and asked how he was. Awkwardly, he shrugged. It was at this point that Lucy decided that it was her job, no duty, to find Steve a girlfriend.

"Get your phone out." She ordered.

Not feeling he had much room to argue, Steve complied.

"Now unlock it."

Again Steve complied.

"Now give it to me."

He handed her the phone.

"I know just the app for you." She quickly found the 'Finders, Keepers' app and downloaded it to his phone. Once it opened, she ran through the sign up process.

"Now I know you're a nice bloke, but we actually want to find you a girlfriend, so I'm going to fill in your profile for you. It'll be mainly the truth, but we don't want to put anyone off do we?"

Steve didn't really know what to say. He didn't like the idea of lying but if it was mainly the truth, then any little misunderstandings could be worked out once they had decided that they like each other. At least that's what he told himself.

Triumphantly, Lucy held the phone aloft and presented him with his newly completed profile. He looked at it. It was mainly true he consoled himself.

"Now take a selfie. Come over here the light's better."

Lucy dragged him into a corner by the dartboard. The ring of light surrounding the board made for an impromptu selfie light. He took a few. Lucy grabbed the phone from his hand and selected the third one.

"There. Now all we need to do is turn it live, aaaand, you're on the market!"

'On the market'. What an awful phrase. He finished his drink and pocketed his phone, waved goodbye to Lucy, who called "Good luck" as he left the pub for his home and meal for one in front of News at Ten.

It was around a week later that he thought to look at the app on his phone. He wasn't really sure how to use it, but he'd been receiving 4 emails a day from 'Finders Keepers' encouraging him to log back in and 'Take a look at all the fresh new members looking for that special kind of love'. Initially he thought he might disable the endless notifications, but on his way to the Settings, he noticed the picture of someone who caused him to stop. His thumb hovered over the image.

Involuntarily, his thumb twitched its agreement, and pressed down on the image, releasing it with a haptic click, her profile sprang into full screen.

A woman in her mid-thirties looked out from his phone. Pretty, in a plain way, she had short dark hair, neat, restrained make up, and soft brown eyes that he felt were looking at him. A pang shot through him. This had never happened before and he paid attention to it.

Beneath her picture there was a big blue button that said 'Connect with Tracy'. He paused, and scanned the info she had provided in her profile. She worked in customer services, also mainly from home. 35, not overweight but not slim, 5'4. He wondered how much he could trust this info, considering the job Lucy had done on his profile.

He looked back at the photo, the pang returned. This time he clicked the blue button, and the phone made a whooshing noise, like a skier flying past you on some freezing downhill slope.

Locking his phone he placed it on it's charger, logged back in to his work and continued with his day.

Later that evening, Tracy picked up her phone and noticed the little red notification icon on the 'Finders' app. Opening it, she was presented with the picture of Steve and the profile that Lucy had crafted for him. Not unattractive or attractive. Lives alone, works from home. On balance not too bad she thought.

Clicking the 'Connect with Steve' button, she typed him a message in the box that was now visible.

"Hi Steve, thanks for liking my profile. Can you tell me a little bit more about yourself please?"

There followed some back and forth between them as they decided if they wanted to meet up. It was decided that they did.

A wet Tuesday in a pub halfway between their houses was to be the meeting place. Steve had finished work early and got himself ready as best he could. He took his comb from his inside jacket pocket, and ran it through his hair. Shaking wisps of brown hair away, he puts it back in his pocket. Leaving his flat, he waits at the bus stop outside his home.

Tracy also stood in front of her mirror. She tugged at the hem of her frock, which was trying to ride up over her knees. She considered changing it, but thought that by the time she had her raincoat on it wouldn't show. She checked the bathroom and turned to leave. Everything was as it should be. She pulled the door to, and left her house for the pub.

Half an hour later after awkward introductions, they sat facing each other, he with a pint of something dark and real and her with a fizzing pint of Somerset's finest. Despite Steve's shyness he managed to find some topics they both seemed interested in and they talked, together for two and a half hours.

"I've got to go soon otherwise I'll miss my bus" Tracy said. "Did you get here by bus?"

Steve nods.

"We can walk together then. Would you like to hold my arm?"

Steve nods again. This is like a proper date. Not some drunken thing his friends seemed to enjoy. This was calm and, well, romantic. Just like the app promised. Taking her arm he led her from the pub to the bus station.

It transpired that they both lived on the same bus route. It was a circular route, so if you stayed on the bus long enough you would go past both of their homes. The bus arrived and they agreed to get on together. Tracy talked and Steve listened until they got near Tracy's house.

"I've had such a nice evening, it would be a shame to end it so early, would you like to come in for a cup of tea and a bite to eat?"

This situation really didn't happen to Steve very often, in fact he couldn't recall this ever having happened before. He looked at her and smiled.

"That's settled then. Come on. She tugged his sleeve as they both scurried downstairs and hopped off the bus together.

It was at that point that Steve missed his footing and tumbled into a massive puddle that ran over the high curb by the bus stop. He went in face first and grazed his wrist as he tried to break his fall.

From the ground he could hear Tracy laughing.

"I'm sorry" she said. "I know it's not funny" offering him a hand she continued "at least this date is memorable!" Taking her hand he got to his feet. He was soaked from head to foot.

"Get inside" she says and motions him in.

Steve wakes. Heavy lidded, he struggles to open his eyes. Something is wrong. Thickly blinking, he smells damp rope, wet hemp. His wrists and ankles tightly bound. There is a gag, taped to his mouth, he tries to panic; breathe freely.

Naked. In a bath. In a strange place. Alone. The silence.

Hot, seriously hot, water is pouring in from the tap at his feet. He struggles to get out, but the bath is too deep and slippery, he can't get any purchase, barely keeping his head above water.

Trying to call out, the gag taped to his face is so expertly applied, he can barely draw breath let alone call for help.

Then from the side of the bath, a head appears. It's Tracy.

"That's better, just had to make a few adjustments. Oh Steve, I'm so glad we met. I'd almost lost hope of finding someone. It's been months since I had someone over."

Now how about that tea? She reaches for the oversized mug and takes a sip.

"Do you like it? The mug I mean"

She dips a hand into the bath water.

"Ooo that's better, still a way to go though."

Dragging a chair from the corner of the bathroom, Tracy settles on it and leaning forward she cradles the cup in both hands.

The water is getting hotter and hotter. Steve lets out a plaintive moan. Small bubbles start to rise from the bottom of the bath and the water temperature continues to rise.

"Now my darling, as I said, it's been a while since I've had anyone over for dinner. The freezer is practically empty."

Steve moans again. The water is so hot now his flesh has started to take on the complexion of a boiled ham.

"I would finish you off, but I find the meat is infinitely tastier if it's braised on a low heat first.

Braise away, braise away, braise away!

I'm assured it doesn't hurt.

After a while. I'm sure you understand."

There is a hiss of gas. Rubbery tubes feed burners under the impromptu cooking pot. Two large gas cylinders stand sentry either side of the tub.

Steam rises from the bath. The water starts to boil.

Steve disappears beneath the roiling water.

Tracy produces a fork from a bathroom drawer and prods at the cooking flesh, teasing a chunk of meat from Steve's chest, she sniffs the fatty flesh, and examines the tattoo still visible on his poached hide. It's a shit tattoo. She takes a bite of Steve.

Tracy eats with her mouth open, talking while she eats, wiping his grease from her chin with her sleeve on the back of her hand.

Sitting in her bathroom, condensation running down the walls, staring at her misted mirror she says to herself

"Lovely."

Three Steps Behind

Snow had come early and heavily this year. It started about a week ago and hadn't really stopped. And so it was, that on Christmas eve, Arno Way found himself trudging through the drifts, on the dreary rundown streets, of the hilly seaside town he called home.

He hated Christmas shopping and only did the absolute minimum, at the last possible minute, in order to satisfy his very limited obligations. Both his parents were dead and he had never married or had children. The only people he felt he needed to buy presents for, were his brother's kids. They were at the age where Christmas still felt magical, so he didn't really mind spending a few quid on them.

Arno thought back warmly to his own childhood. He remembered the trouble his parents had gone to on Christmas eve: the stockings full of presents, carefully left at the foot of the bed, the notes to Santa, burnt, smoke up the chimney, a carrot for Rudolph, the mince pie and tumbler of whisky left as payment for Santa's fleeting visit.

A recent dump of snow had made driving hazardous, so he parked his car closer to the top of the hill, rather than attempt to get down the steep gradient into town. There were enough abandoned cars on the streets as it was, he didn't need to add his to the cluttered kerbs.

A few hours later, night was falling and it started snowing heavily once again. Arno turned his back on the Christmas lights and sounds of the shops, and struggled up the hill, laden with the gifts he'd spent the afternoon buying.

The sudden flurry and freezing wind, cleared the streets and Arno found himself cresting the hill alone. It was then that he spotted something through the blizzard.

Ahead of him was one of the town's bridges, crossing the turbulent gorge, separating the old town in the east, from the new development in the west. The bridge was of Victorian construction, originally painted pale corporation blue; rust now pockmarked the cast iron lattices forming the railings. White lamp posts punctuated the barrier, holding dim lights aloft, the protective glass, cracked and uncared for.

Around one lamp post, still in possession of a working bulb, near the centre of the bridge, Arno could make out the shape of something, no someone, climbing over the rail, into harm's way.

Arno stepped from the shadows and called out,

"Hey there, are you OK?"

The dark figure turned towards him. It was a woman, clinging to the post with only one hand. She was wildly inappropriately dressed for such a bitter and windswept evening. With no coat, and wearing only a thin nightdress, she started to flap her free arm at him, as if to wave him away. Arno took another step forward. The woman started shouting at him, "Go back! Go away!"

"What are you doing? You're going to fall!" He took another few steps towards her.

"Go back! You don't know what you're doing!" She was becoming more agitated.

Arno stopped. Maybe he could reason with her. "Let's talk about whatever it is. I'm sure I can help you!"

"No one can help me. There's no more to be done!" She looked away for a moment. Arno took a few steps closer to the distraught woman. Almost within touching distance, Arno stretched out a hand; he had a fingertip on the woman's arm when she suddenly snapped her head around and stared him straight in the eye.

Arno had never seen a look like this before in any eye. Her pupils were coal black and filled their sockets. A small tear of deep red blood began to trickle down her cheek. She snarled a thin lipped grimace before shrieking at him "I warned you to stay away!" Her bellow was such an unearthly howl, it stopped the blood in his veins, anaesthetised, he was frozen to the spot.

The woman hissed at him and grabbed his wrist with both hands. Slipping from her perch, safety fell away from beneath her, as she dangled above the tumultuous ravine. The grip she had on him was the only thing between life and certain death in the freezing waters below. Arno braced himself against the edge of the bridge, taking the strain.

In an instant, her expression changed. Suddenly, a woman in her fifties, her life hanging by a thread, eyes no longer black and lifeless, looked back pitifully at him. Mouthing "I'm sorry," she relaxed her grip on his wrists. At the moment she let go of his arm, Arno felt something pass between them, his lungs spasmed a puff of freezing air across his larynx. He recoiled, as she receded into the darkness, onto the rocks and down into the tumbling river below.

Arno stood for a second. "Had that really just happened?" The heavy snow wiped clean traces of the woman's passage to the bridge, the raging river swept away any remaining evidence of her existence. He reached for his phone. "Call the p-police," he stammered to himself. He dug down into the pocket he reserved solely for his phone. It wasn't there.

Thinking back, he pictured himself leaving the house. He had been heading towards the door, when his brother had called him to tell him they would be out through the day, but back by around six that evening.

He wanted to get the kids ready for bed nice and early, as it was always a struggle to get them to sleep on Christmas eve.

Suddenly, realising how little time he had to do his Christmas shopping, Arno had gathered up his hat, coat, gloves, and keys and abruptly left the house, leaving his phone on the kitchen table. So busy had he been shopping, that up until this moment, he hadn't realised it was missing.

"Damn," he thought to himself. He looked around. He wasn't overly familiar with the eastern part of town, he only ever drove mindlessly through it, on his way to the shops. "I wonder if there's any pubs around here?" It was properly dark now and the shops would all be closed for the holidays. A pub might be the quickest place to go to, to alert the police. He went to search for the nearest one, but then remembered he didn't have his stupid phone.

Looking around, there was little sign of life. This bit of town mostly comprised of industrial units and greasy spoons that closed early on a work day, let alone on Christmas eve. He thought about investigating his surroundings further, but reasoned it would be quicker if he made his way back to the car and headed straight to his brother's.

Picking up the gifts, he hurried as fast as he could through the mounting piles of snow. Once he reached the car, he opened the boot and put the presents in. He took off his coat and gave it a good shake to dislodge the icy dandruff that settled on his shoulders; he threw it on top of everything else, slamming the lid shut. He climbed into his freezing car and started the engine. Setting the heater to maximum, he moved to turn the wipers on. Looking up, he realised there was no way they would clear the amount of snow on the windscreen, so, leaving the engine running, he got out and used his gloved hands to clear what he could from the windows.

Working his way around the vehicle, he eventually got back to the driver's door, and was just about to get in, when he noticed an extra set of prints in the snow. "That's odd," he thought; it was difficult to tell what had made them, as he had trodden over the top of them, he assumed maybe a dog. "I don't remember seeing a dog running around here," he looked again, "and such a big dog!" He stopped to ponder for a moment, until the bitter chill got the better of him and he slid back into the freezing driver's seat.

His car was quite old and it hated cold weather. On frosty mornings, he was never quite sure if it would go at all, so he was very pleased it started at the first time of asking, especially now, when he'd really needed it to.

As the engine idled, he sniffed at the air. "What was that awful smell?" He sniffed again. A foul stench was slowly filling his car. He opened the window. It must have been five below outside, but the smell was so bad, he tolerated the cold momentarily. "Must be something on the industrial estate," he mused.

Finally, he was ready to set off for his brother's house, a drive that would normally take him no more than ten minutes from where he'd parked, but now, with conditions as they were, he'd already been driving for fifteen and wasn't even half way there yet. He pulled up at the set of red traffic lights that always seemed to catch him.

He thought about the woman. Her eyes were just so odd and the sudden change in her character, so weird. It had taken up to this point, for Arno to really appreciate just how strange the encounter had been. He shuddered slightly at the thought of it, however, it was not the thought of the poor dead woman that made the hackles on Arno's neck stand on end, it was the sensation of warm moist breath blowing about his ears that made him clench.

Arno spun around in his seat and clutched at the back of his neck. Was there something there? The dog from earlier? Perhaps it had jumped into the car while he was clearing the snow. He felt for his phone again. "Bugger." He reached for the inside light and tried to switch it on. "Bloody thing," he muttered.

He kept meaning to get it fixed, but never seemed to find the time, besides, he always carried his phone, the torch was usually good enough.

The traffic light cycled through red to amber to green and Arno decided it wasn't a massive surprise that he might be a bit spooked, considering the events of the evening so far. Pulling away, he made for his brother's.

Fifteen minutes later, Arno arrived at the festive front door. The snow had picked up in intensity, as had the wind, which scoured the street before him. Racing around to the boot of the car, Arno opened it and grabbed the unwrapped presents. Slamming the hatch shut, he ran up the path and rang the doorbell. After a short pause, the hall light came on and a man in his late thirties answered. Arno pushed his way past, and made his way into the warm.

Arno's brother was used to being shoved around by his younger sibling. He was about to close the front door, when he hesitated for an instant.

"Shut the door, it's freezing!"

"Sorry," he replied. "I thought I saw something."

"Well I saw something tonight that's left me properly shaken, I can tell you. But before I tell you, you need to shut the front door and I need to borrow your phone."

Arno's brother pointed to the phone in the hall; Arno sat down at the table it rested on and very deliberately stabbed out 999 on the keypad.

....

Forty minutes later, Arno places the receiver back in its holder. All the while his brother has been listening intently.

"Bloody hell! That was a bit off! Are the police coming round?" he asks.

"Yes, as soon as they can."

"When's that?"

"It's Christmas eve. You tell me."

Arno stands and stretches. "Can I use the bathroom Bruv? I'm busting."

"Sure, you know where it is," Arno's brother sniffs the air, "and you might want to check your shoes. Smells like you've trodden in something horrible."

Arno finishes his piss and zips up. He washes his hands in the sink and splashes his face with warm water. What a strange day he's having. Right next to the sink is a towel rail, he can feel its heat on his face as he dries his hands and dabs at his forehead on the light blue towel stretched over the radiator. He moves to check himself in the mirror. "Oops, forgot to flush." He turns and reaches for the chain and flushes, he spins back toward the mirror, except he doesn't get that far. On the light blue towel, next to the damp marks where he dried himself, there are another set of unexpected marks. Arno claps a hand to his mouth. The marks on the towel are more like prints, huge wet paw prints. He takes a step backwards and notices the bath mat in front of him ruffle slightly. Taking another step, he sees the impression of a footprint appear in the pile of the mat.

Grabbing the towel, he backs very slowly out of the bathroom and makes for the kitchen. His brother has wooden floors throughout his house and with every backward step Arno makes, he can hear the sound of another footfall, three steps behind him.He continues to walk down the passageway.

The footsteps follow, trip, trap, trip, trap.

Occasionally he gets a strong whiff of something horrible, something rotting, something putrid, something dead.

Just as he crosses the kitchen, the children find him. "Uncle Arno, Uncle Arno, it's nearly Christmas!!" They jump up and down on the spot in front of him, waving their arms about, as children do.

Arno looks over their heads, directly and very intently at his brother. "I need to have a word with you, in private, NOW!"

Arno's brother only has to take one look at Arno's face to know this is serious.

"Shall we go to my office?"

"No, here. We must talk here."

"Ok children, your uncle and I need to have a word, so can you both go back into the front room and play for a bit please?"

They both seem a bit deflated "Hawww," they say in unison, their shoulders slump a little. "NOW! Please. Don't forget Santa's watching." He points first to his eyes and then at them. They hop to attention and scamper out of the room.

Arno's brother shuts the door.

"What is it? You look like you've seen a ghost!"

"It's not a ghost."

"What do you mean, not a ghost? Is there something then? What is it?"

"I don't know Bruv but I think something's following me. Something vile and not very friendly. You know what I said about the woman's eyes and how they changed from dead to pitiful?

It was as if something had suddenly decided to leave her. Whatever had been tormenting her suddenly relaxed its grip. In that moment, I felt something pass between us. Then this just happened."

Arno holds the towel out in front of him. His brother takes a moment to work out what he's looking at.

"What have you done to that towel?"

"Look at my hands Bruv." He holds them up before him. They are ever so slightly shaking. He presses one onto one of the marks. The mark is bigger and a completely different shape to his own hand. "See, there's no way I could have made these marks. I think it was this thing, the thing that's following me. I can feel the stench of its breath on the back of my neck and it's getting closer and closer. I can sense it starting to bear down on me."

His brother was just about to speak, when in burst the children. They were fighting over a pot of glitter they were using to decorate Christmas cards.

"It's my turn!"

"No it isn't, you've had your turn!"

Something has to give, in the tug of war between them. It is the pot. The lid flies off and the contents land like a glitter grenade, covering the entire kitchen floor.

Arno snatches the towel away and looks at his brother. "Get them out of here now!"

Arno shifts his body ever so slightly. Unnervingly, two steps behind him, the very clear outline of a foot appears, edged in glitter.

"Daddy? What's that?!" Arno's niece points at the track in the glitter. They all stare in silence at the footprint.

Arno takes half a step forward and the outline takes half a step toward Arno.

"Kids. Front room. Now!" Arno's brother quickly ushers the children into the sitting room. They both start to cry. He shouts "Stay here!" and slams the door shut behind him. He turns to his brother and says, "I don't know what's going on, but whatever it is, I don't want the kids involved. You need to leave. Now. Go home. I'll try to find someone to look after the children and then come over, OK? But right now you need to be somewhere else!"

Arno doesn't feel very much like being on his own with the thing that's stalking him, but he realises he can't stay here. He turns for the front door. His brother stares in horror as Arno is followed by what are clearly two footprints, walking their way through the glitter, a little less than two steps behind him. With a backward glance at his brother, Arno gathers all his courage, lifts a hand to the lock, flips it open and takes a step outside into the night.

It's stopped snowing for the moment, Arno makes the short distance from the house to his car in record time. He dives in and slams the door shut. Rubbing a small circle of condensation from the window, he peers through the watery smear. The footprints are there in the snow behind him, at least they're not still in the house, he thinks to himself. They seem to stop slightly short of the car. Quickly he reaches round and feels for his seat belt. Maybe he's beaten it into the car. Fumbling for the belt, he takes another look outside. Yes they definitely look like they didn't reach this far. He grabs the belt and plunges the tongue into the buckle,

He turns the ignition. A deep, heavy, pungent breath tickles the nape of his neck. Not daring to look round, his head sinks, turtle like into his shoulders, he frantically fumbles to start the car. Panicking, Arno puts his foot flat to the floor. The car careers toward the other side of the road, skidding on the ice and snow.

Gone now is any idea of going home, he must just get away.

Arno drives through abandoned streets weaving this way and that, He checks the rearview mirror. Two red eyes stare back at him. A ravening jaw pants clouds of rancid breath into the chill.

It's so close now, Arno's head is almost pressing on the steering wheel. He can feel its hands at his shoulder, foul saliva, running down his neck, dripping into his shirt.

It's snowing again. Arno can drive no more. Skidding to a halt, he crashes into a line of abandoned cars. His door is jammed, bent by the crash. He shoulder barges it and turns to kick it open, so desperate is he to get out. The door gives way and he falls out into the freezing street. Struggling to get to his feet and slipping on the snow, Arno is doing his best to run, but the beast at his back is pushing him down, enveloping him, its arms around his waist, licking his ear. Vile breath blinding his senses. It is upon him. His eyes blacken as it enters his body and starts to feast.

Blindly staggering on, Arno finds himself at the cast iron bridge with the corporation blue iron lattice and dimly lit lamp posts. Below, the river rages on unabated. Reaching the railing, he clambers over the ironwork and into harm's way. There's still a bit of Arno the beast has not yet devoured; with the last of his humanity, he resolves to take the monster with him, over the edge, smashing them both onto the rocks below. Arno clambers desperately over the edge. Through the heavy snowfall, steps the figure of a man.

He waves at Arno. Arno doesn't see him. The man advances. Arno clutches at the metalwork with one hand, and is just about to let go when he spots the rapidly advancing stranger. The little bit left of Arno Way frantically waves him back. The man calls out,

"Hey there, are you OK?"

The Capsule

It was the day before Thanksgiving aboard the Space Station. Processing around the globe for nearly twenty years, it was now reaching the end of its working life. Only two people remained on board, Kwasi Stephenson and Marissa Ruby. They had been tasked with the job of decommissioning the ageing vessel, and preparing it for a controlled re-entry through the earth's atmosphere, where it would burn up. The remaining parts, falling harmlessly, into the Pacific Ocean.

Marissa and Kwasi were tasked with working their way through an extremely long checklist of items to be saved from obliteration. Over the years there had been a lot of scientific experiments conducted aboard the space station, some of which were top secret, and these had to be carefully accounted for. The Agency didn't want there to be even a remote chance that these might survive re-entry and be recovered by hostile actors.

So it was that the last two astronauts aboard carefully catalogued and stowed any remnants of the experiments on their list, ready for the return to earth.

"Right, let's get to it" Said Kwasi, "We won't be home in time for Easter at this rate."

He picked up the check list. It was all going to plan and they only had one thing left to look at before they could pack up their belongings, and ready themselves for the return journey.

"Marissa, can you show where 17.426 is supposed to be? I can't see it."

Marissa, took the instructions for retrieving the experiment out of a plastic ring binder, and held it up to the light. Squinting slightly, she slowly reads aloud.

"Experiment 17.426; The effects of microgravity on bacterial microbes over an extended period of time."

"Wow! This is an old one. It's been running almost from the start."

"These are some very special microbes," Kwasi jokes.

"They certainly are or rather were. I can't see any sign of them. What exactly am I looking for?"

"Well, it says here that there should be a small incubator, with a few sealed flasks inside. Apparently, the bacteria are anaerobic and self-sustaining."

Marissa peers into a small enclave containing several incubators.

"Hang on there's only one incubator switched on. It's right at the back." Marissa stretches to reach it. The lack of gravity was making reaching for things very difficult.

Marissa stretches toward the catch and pings it open, recoiling slightly as she does. A small light pops on inside the box.

"Three flasks. Should be right in front of you." Kwasi says as he peruses the notes.

"Err nope. Nothing here. Are you sure this is it?"

"Wait, there's a label on the inside of the door. 17.426"

"They should be in there"

"That's as maybe, but if you can see it, you're doing better than me."

Both the crew investigate the inside of the fridge. It's clearly empty.

"I think we'd better call this in."

Marissa pushes away from the corner and floats over to the Comms panel and grabs a headset. Depressing a button on the console. She calls out, "Hey "Mission Control. We've got a bit of a problem here. We're missing a sample."

There is a momentary pause before Cap Com crackles back down the radio "Which is the sample you're missing?"

"The last one. 17.426"

There's a further pause. "Hang on please."

"That's a bit odd." Marissa mumbles.

Kwasi replies, "It is, isn't it? Usually, they're straight back at you if there's a problem"

It was at this point that there was a very loud piercing whistle that came over the radio, which caused Marissa to rip the headset from her ears.

"Jesus! What was that? It almost burst my bloody eardrum!"

"You ok?" Kwasi pushes himself toward her and gingerly picks up the headset and holds it a few centimetres from his ear. "Come in Mission Control. Do you copy?"

All he can hear is the empty hiss of static. "It's dead."

"It can't be. Try the backup"

He switches to the auxiliary radio. Holding the headset slightly away from his ear, just in case, he tries again. "Come in Mission Control". More static. It's dead too.

"How can this be possible? We can't be up here with no radio."

"What about the radio in the shuttle?" says Kwasi.

"Good thinking" Marissa says as she pushes off from the desk and heads toward the capsule. Undoing the airlock, she glides into the vessel and straps herself into the pilot's seat. Flicking a few switches, she turns on the power, lighting up the control panel in front of her.

She takes the headset from its stowage and carefully holds it a few centimetres from her ear. "Cap Com do you read me? Come in Mission Control." She releases the talk button and waits for a reply.

Kwasi drops in behind her. "Well?"

She slowly lowers the headset. "Nothing. Not even static. Just dead air."

"Did you have to put it like that?"

"Sorry."

"What are we going to do?"

"Do you know, I really don't know. We never simulated three radios going down at the same time. Why would we?"

"Well regardless of that, they have. How are we going to get home?"

They both stare at each other in silence. From the main module there comes a loud crash. "What the hell was that?"

Kwasi is the first to move, he pushes off hard and heads back into the capsule.

He is greeted by the sight of the radio tumbling and bashing off the walls of the craft.

It has been ripped from the console, wires dangle freely in space. Marissa is right behind him.

They both stare in horror at the sight before them.

"Is it fixable?"

"Does it look fixable? It's knackered. More to the point, how did it end up here?"

Marissa catches hold of the wrecked radio and they both stare at it.

After a pause Marissa turns to Kwasi.

"You were in here on your own. Did you do it?"

"Of course I didn't bloody do it. Why would I? Do you think I really want to die up here? We both heard the bang! Didn't we?"

Marissa thinks for a moment. Even though the incident only happened a few seconds ago, she's struggling to remember. "Yes, yes I suppose so."

"Marissa, what do you mean 'I suppose so'? Marissa, look at me. Look at me. We were there together when we heard the bang. We were in the capsule together. Remember? Marissa?"

Marissa shakes her head and tries to remember.

"C'mon Marissa. I need you to be 100% in the room. We're in a lot of trouble and I can't do this on my own."

"It's ok. I'm ok." She regained her composure and took a deep breath. "I'm fine."

Kwasi floated up to the control panel and took down two large ring binders. These were the procedures for returning the capsule to earth.

"What are you doing Kwasi?"

"I'm making a decision; we're going to have to leave the ship. We've got no radio and I'm concerned about you. If we leave it much longer, I don't know what's going to happen."

"But I'm the ranking officer here, we've got a mission to complete. You can't just…"

Her voice drifts off and a far-off look comes over her.

"Marissa! Marissa! Snap out of it! For Christ's sake! Marissa!"

Marissa's body grows limp, her arms drift in front of her, shoulders rising above her drooping head, she rests, as if drowned in mid-air. Kwasi pushes himself over to her. Holding her head, he lifts it and looks in her eyes. They are open and she is breathing, but she looks out of it. Kwasi does a slow orbit of his comatose colleague. Grabbing the scruff of her neck he pushes off and drags her to the tool locker. Opening it with his free hand he rummages around inside until he finds the duct tape. Biting the end, he pulls a long strip out and begins to wind it around Marissa's unconscious body. He loops the tape around a strut several times tethering her to the ship.

Kwasi finds the manuals and takes them to the capsule. Entering the module for the last time he opens a locker and removes two space suits.

At this point Marissa begins to stir.

"Kwasi, what's going on?" She slowly starts to come to, discovering her bindings, she struggles to move. "What's going on? Kwasi. Kwasi! Kwasi untie me!"

"Don't be silly Marissa!" He chuckled. "Why would I do that?"

"Kwasi, have you lost your mind?"

"Oh yes Marissa. I have, quite completely."

"What?" She shook her head again and struggled to free herself, but the tape held its grip.

"The experiment 17.426. You know what? It worked!" He looks at her as she struggles against her bonds.

He continues, "The purpose of 17.426 was to see what effect long term microgravity had on bacteria. Well, the effect was that over time, they mutated. These weren't any ordinary bacteria to start with; they were a culture that had been engineered by the military. They have this really weird property, whereby, contact with them would cause a sudden personality change in the exposed subject. They would become very aggressive and almost uncontrollable with rage. The experiment was to see if they could be engineered to keep the aggression but make the host more receptive to commands, and it worked, sort of."

"But why does that involve smashing the radio and tying me up? Couldn't we have just taken it back together?"

"That was the plan, but unfortunately, I've been got at by the other side. I've been an agent for them for years. Getting picked for this mission was what I had been tasked with. I knew I couldn't get the flask past you. So you know what I did? I infected myself with a sample. I ditched the rest out the airlock, into space. I've got an endless supply of the bacterium sloshing around in my veins now. Aside from making me quite angry, 14.426 has also given me a very strong desire to survive. Overwhelmingly so in fact, and now you know about me, you must die. Sorry old love. That's just how it is."

"So now I'm going to fake an accident, where you die, and I return to earth alone as the sole survivor. Obviously, I'll be the hero."

"You bloody lunatic! Let me go!"

"Goodbye Marissa. I do hope you'll burn up completely. I wouldn't want any evidence to be left." and with that he reached into the tool box and removes a knife. He takes

Marissa's space suit, holds it up and slashes a large hole in it. He grins broadly at her, abandoning the knife he enters the capsule and winds the air lock shut.

Through the cupola she could see the external lights of the capsule flicker on as Kwasi went through the steps to ready the capsule for re-entry.

This wasn't quite how she'd imagined her final minutes, trussed up, alone and helpless in space.

She glances around for anything that might help her free herself of the tape. At that moment, she notices the knife Kwasi had so carelessly discarded, slowly pirouetting towards her. As it gets closer, she manages to wriggle a few fingers free on her bonds and stretches her fingertips toward the blade of the knife as it slowly processes past her.

Just as it arrives at her hand, she catches the very end of the blade. She lets out a breath, "Don't drop it", she says to herself, as she instantly fumbles it. "Shit it!" she hisses.

Dropping the knife has changed its trajectory, and with the first bit of luck she'd had that day, it spins towards her head. Very carefully, she catches the handle in her mouth. She takes a breath. Using her tongue and teeth she adjusts her grip on the knife, and sets about sawing at the tape around her neck. After a minute, despite stabbing herself a few times, she manages to work her shoulders free.

Kwasi is getting near to the end of the checklist and he will soon be leaving.

Marissa gets one arm almost out of her bindings. With a final heave her arm is free. She grabs the knife from her mouth and quickly frees the rest of her body from the remaining tape.

Flying to the cupola she can see Kwasi is on the last few steps of the re-entry procedure. She must act fast. But what can she do? She knows she is doomed. Even if she can get him out of the capsule, she doesn't have a suit for re-entry, he's destroyed hers and his won't fit her. Without it, she will almost certainly suffocate on the way back down. No, there is nothing left to do except for something desperate and she needs to do it fast!

It was at that moment that Kwasi releases the capsule from the mothership. It silently parts company and starts to turn toward the Earth. She can see the thrusters blinking in the darkness as the capsule begins to recede into the distance.

She looks at the control panel. What was she going to do? She scans it again. "Wait," she says to herself. "There are thrusters on this ship too!"

There was no time for procedure. All she can do is to have one burn of the engines. One chance. Marissa has always been an outstandingly intuitive pilot. She had been top of any class she had been in, and now was the time for her to show what she was really made of. Tracking Kwasi's capsule on the radar to her left, she quickly calculates and punches his trajectory into the main guidance computer and sets the space station on a collision course with the capsule. Locking in the coordinates she was just about to hit the button for a full and final burn when she hesitates. "What if I miss?" She adjusts the fuel so she saves a tiny amount just in case. With that she smashes her hands down on the fire button and the huge space ship vibrates and heaves as it begins to move.

There is enough fuel for a thirty second burn at full thrust. The space station picks up speed as the monstrous vehicle lumbers into action. The angle she's been forced to set means that if she misses Kwasi she will bounce off the earth's atmosphere and head off into deep space, never to be seen again. She hangs onto the control panel as the giant engines push the station toward the capsule.

Her head drops slightly as she considers her fate, but the risk of letting him get back down to the ground with the mutated bacteria inside him was not something she could allow.

She notices that she has been running a temperature for quite some time. Her teeth were clamped together and she wasn't feeling herself. Then it dawned on her, the strange feeling she'd experienced, the passing out. She must have been infected too. She redoubles her determination to stop Kwasi at any cost.

The space station has now picked up considerable speed and is bearing down on Kwasi's ship. Through the cupola she can see the capsule grow and in the window of the escape pod, Kwasi's face as they speed toward each other. She can see him frantically calculating adjustments to his path to avoid being rammed.

Marissa has already taken this into account. From where they are, she calculates there is only one escape trajectory that doesn't involve Kwasi's destruction by the huge satellite. But would he try to take it? Kwasi was an adequate pilot at best, and Marissa reasons he will find it and try to take it, but it will take split second timing, and she still has one last trick up her sleeve.

She can see the thrusters on the capsule ignite for a final desperate burn as Kwasi attempts to escape.

"Got you" says Marissa as she fires the rockets, they splutter back into life, there's just enough fuel to change course, and the Space Station turns just enough to clip the capsule, nudging Kwasi's ship, flipping it so the heat shield is no longer protecting it from the destructive heat of re-entry. Through the glass Marissa can see Kwasi, pressed against the window, his fists hammering on the glass, his face contorted in rage as the capsule glows red, then white hot, as he winks out of existence.

Meanwhile, the lumbering space station gently bounces off the earth's atmosphere as it slowly spins into the vast emptiness of space.

At that point the back-up radio spits back into life.

"Space station, do you copy. Come in. Do you copy?"

But Marissa doesn't copy. She simply stares from the cupola back at the fast-receding Earth, whilst a quiet bacterial rage boils away inside her.

37 Lombard Street

Devotnic Butkas parks outside the large glass and steel facade of the newly renovated offices in London's Lombard Street. The building has had many incarnations in its long history, formerly part of the offices of the East India Company, its anonymous facade hid a beautifully restored and modernised interior. She presses her phone to the front door lock which clicks open and she makes her way through a narrow archway and out into the main body of the building.

So extensive had the renovations been that a time traveller familiar with the building's past, would have found it difficult to tell exactly where they were. A new bright atrium had been carved from the existing floors and a glass cupola allowed shafts of light to penetrate deep within the building.

Devotnic stood for a moment and took in the sight. When her company had been appointed architects to undertake the renovation, the building had been entirely different. Where now stood the bright atrium, there had been a greasy unreliable lift. It had sliding lattice shutters instead of solid doors, so you always felt you were going to lose at least one finger every time you used it. The lift would break down at least once a week, usually on a Friday around 2pm, when a few of the more dissolute staff would come back from the pub and cram into it, causing it to get stuck between floors. The very unhappy fire brigade would turn up an hour or so later to free and chide the inhabitants, who now were seriously in need of the toilet.

It had been an easy decision to rip the lift out and start again. She had installed a modern glass elevator at the back of the building. It filled the entirety of the tiny courtyard garden, which had up until then, been the smoking area. Almost no one smoked now and sympathy for those who still did, had long since been extinguished. Smoking was completely banned, even from outside the building. A few harboured a resentment over this but fewer bothered mentioning it.

Devotnic was due to meet her chief electrician there that Sunday afternoon. He'd had to drive in from deepest Essex and would have come in the Morning but for the fact that he had attended the christening of his nephew. He could hardly have skipped it, what with him being the kids godfather and all.

Somewhat begrudgingly he had agreed to meet Devotnic in the afternoon. The rest of the family were having a proper party. Weddings, christenings, and funerals, his lot knew how to do a do. He had considered cancelling, but Dev as he called her, was an important customer whose projects were worth serious money to him. The work had allowed his family to build a successful business off the back of the contracts.

Initially, some had been resistant to working for Dev.

"Another bloody immigrant coming over here stealing our jobs…"

"Who the bloody hell does she think she is?"

"Bloody Poles".

Except DevotnicButkas wasn't Polish or Romanian, she was very definitely Lithuanian. Arriving in Britain as a young woman, essentially penniless, she had worked for years on building sites, labouring for minimum wage through the day, and studying by night at the Open University, learning to be an architect. Not only had she put herself through the course, she also sent what money she could home to her widowed mother in Vilnius. After seven long years of hard graft, Devotnic had not only qualified as an architect but she had also built up a huge number of contacts in the London building trade.

The labouring had allowed her to work on a tremendous number of projects and get to know how you did things in London. So, it hadn't taken her long to get a start in her new career. At first it was a few subcontracting jobs, designing a stairway or assisting with the groundwork. After a time, these smaller jobs progressed to larger and more important work. Finally, she landed the Lombard Street job two years ago. The removal of the lift and the addition of the atrium was what had swung the contract for her. It was bright and bold and there wasn't anything else like it in the surrounding streets. It had persuaded the property's owners to keep the building's facade rather than tear it down for yet another anonymous office block.

And now here she was on the eve of her triumph, the opening of the building and the arrival of the tenants. From behind her she could hear a card being swiped and a door unlocking as the electrician made his way into the building.

"Dev" he called, waving an arm at her and carrying a clipboard under the other. As the work had yet to be fully signed off, they were both wearing hard hats. Dev tipped her's towards the electrician heading toward her.

"Afternoon, sorry about that. The insurance company won't sign them off until we double check the wiring for the new lift. I don't know why they're being so picky."

"It might be something to do with the tube line that runs about 20 feet below the basement! Can't be having any accidents down there can we now?"

They both roll their eyes at each other in the now traditional "Health and safety gone mad" way, everybody on a building sight is obliged to do. Neither of them wants there to be any room for doubt or accidents, so despite their seeming reticence to comply, they both happily do so.

"Shall we get started then?" Dev asks.

"Might as well, I might even make it back in time for a bit of cake!"

Devotnic laughs, and they head to the back of the building. She takes a set of keys from her pocket and approaches a large slab of marble that forms one of the walls. She feels for the special spot and gently presses it. With a satisfying clunk, a small flap springs open, and a handle with a keyhole is revealed. She takes the keys and sorts through them, finding the correct one, she inserts it into the lock turning it one full rotation. Devotnic removes the key and grasps the handle, twisting it, she releases the catch that's been holding the marble slab in place and the huge door swings effortlessly open.

"OO that's very satisfying" says the electrician.

Devotnic gives a small chuckle to herself. "Craftswomanship" she replies.

Behind the door there lies a stairway. This isn't the stairway to the basement. The basement has a cafe in it and a small gym. No, this stairway is the stairway to the level below the basement. It's slightly bigger than a crawl space but you can just stand fully upright in it.

Devotnic pulls a torch from her inside pocket, and flicks it on. They both begin the descent. Despite the safety lighting Devotnic keeps her torch on. The stairs are very narrow and steep; they also curl around to the right as they wind round the walls of the basement.

They had originally wanted to put a trap door in the floor of the cafe so they could improve the access to the sub-basement but Building Control were having none of it. As soon as you got within 50 feet of a tube line you were pretty much required to work on the floor with an archaeologists' trowel and a toothbrush. You were also on the hook for any financial implications of your work. Not wanting to be bankrupted by a trapdoor, Devotnic had decided to utilise the existing access.

The electrician had cursed the decision every single day that he and his team had been forced to carry a lot of heavy electrical equipment down by hand, into the hot void below the cafe. But they had done so, and now the fruits of their labour were now standing before them.

"That's sure some pretty wiring"

"Thanks, Dev. It should be, you know how much time and effort it took to get that lot down here."

"I surely do! Now let's take a look at what the insurance company is going on about shall we?"

The Electricians lifted his clipboard and Dev shone the torch at the paperwork. They began to flick through the pages

"Ah here it is. Section 13b." They both studied the section that had been ringed in red.

"I'm not sure what they mean exactly by this" said the Electrician.

"Doesn't this relate to the lift?"

"No, that's 12 C,D,E and F. I don't recall there being a section 13 at all. To be honest section 13 usually gets left off altogether, superstition being where it is in the building trade"

They look again.

"Where's section 13a?" Say's Dev

"There isn't one"

"Are you sure?"

"It's not in their paperwork and it's all I've got"

Dev sighs. "Right, well, we had better check what we have got"

They look again and there is a diagram in the notes that neither of them had noticed before.

"Where did that come from?"

The electrician shrugs.

It is a diagram, apparently of the space they are standing in. To the right of the patch panel, they were admiring, the diagram indicates a smaller recessed door.

At that moment the ground beneath them starts to rumble and the floor begins to shake. They are both exceedingly familiar with the approach of the DLR train heading toward the Monument; it stops the conversation as they wait for it to pass.

"Wait, there's no door there" says the electrician, I've practically lived down here for the last year and believe me I would have noticed"

Devotnic, flashes the torch at where the diagram indicates the presence of a door.

They both are shocked to see, under the torches harsh white light, a small recessed door.

"Is this some kind of joke, Dev? Because if it is, I'm not finding it very funny."

"No, I swear. I don't know how this can be. Where did you get those documents?"

"They were hand delivered to my site office. I thought you'd sent them."

"No, I swear, the first I knew about it was when you told me about the documents in your text the other day, and we arranged to meet here today."

They both stood in an uncomfortable silence for a moment.

"Well? What are we going to do? We can't ignore it now we've found it."

Devotnic hesitated for an instant. She put a hand on the electrician's arm.

"Wait" she said.

"What's the matter, it's only a door?"

Devotnic, felt the colour drain from her face. Her breath quickened and she steadied herself on the wall.

"Are you OK? You're as white as a sheet"

"In my country, as a child we get told tales about things like this. It sounded ridiculous to think such things could happen in days and times like these, but seeing this has stirred up a memory I have. I once saw a door like this."

"Dev, this is not a great time to start telling me fairy stories."

"It's not a fairy story." She pauses. "It's about the Baubas."

"The what?"

"The Baubas. When you want children to be good you threaten them with the Baubas. They have long thin arms and long thin fingers with great long nails. They have bright red eyes and hide under your bed, or behind your cupboards and grab you if you've been naughty. I'm trying to think of the English name for them."

"The bogeyman?" The electrician offers.

"Yes, yes that's it. The bogeyman"

"Brilliant. Are you trying to tell me the bogeyman lives behind that door?"

"I don't know. All I know is that when I was 8 years old, a door, just like this one, appeared in my brother's bedroom one night. He was younger than me and he called me in to look at it because he was so scared. We couldn't call our parents because that would only make it worse. Part of the story was that if you told, the Baubas would come back and find you later and things would be a lot worse for you"

"Did you tell them? Dev, did you?"

Devotnic, swallows uncomfortably. "Yes, I told them. I ran downstairs and got them to come and take a look. By the time they had returned to my brother's bedroom, the door had gone, and so had he."

"Are you trying to tell me this is true? What happened to your brother?"

"I don't know. My parents were distraught, my father especially, they looked and looked and looked for him but no trace was ever found. My father died of a broken heart a year later. My mother blamed me for my brother's disappearance and my father's death. That's why I left Lithuania. I came here to make a fresh start but now it looks like it's found me."

The electrician looked at Devotnic. He couldn't be sure what to make of Dev's tale.

"Dev, there must be some other explanation for this. Monsters aren't real. I'm really sorry about your brother, but maybe he wandered off and the door was just a dream. This is London 2024. Stuff like that just doesn't happen here. I'm going to show you."

He moves toward the door.

"No, don't. It feels like it's happening again. Please leave it. We must go."

"Look I don't believe in ghosts and neither should you" the electrician stretches out a hand and gives the door a shove. It doesn't move. He turns and wrestles the torch out of Dev's hand. Scanning the surface of the door he notices a small handle in the middle of the left-hand side. He takes a breath and grasps the handle. Turning it, he gives the door another shove. This time it gives. He shoves it again; it swings fully open. A curl of dust follows its path.

"Please don't. Close it! Close it!" The main lights in the sub-basement flicker and fail as another tube train approaches and the room rattles and shakes.

The Electrician ignores her, "I'm going to show you there's nothing here but some superstitions you need to get over" and shines the light into inky blackness.

From within the gloom, two red eyes stare back and a long spindly arm with long tearing claws shoots out and grabs for the door. Reflexively he throws the torch at the thing and slams the door shut.

The lights have gone out, a thick darkness surrounds them, neither of them speak. The floor begins to vibrate as a train approaches. The lights flicker in time to the rhythm of train on track..

In the blinking light Devotnic notices a figure in the shadows. A long thin clawed arm unfolds in her direction. Dev tries to speak, but the words catch in her throat. She waves a hand at the electrician. He sees her and turns to look at what she is now pointing at. In the flickering light a pair of red eyes blink at them.

"Dev, we need to go."

Devotnic nods, her childhood fears now a haunting reality. They turn to leave, but the sub-basement seems to have transformed into an unfamiliar maze. The room rumbles as another train passes underneath their feet, the sound seems distant and they struggle to keep their balance as thier senses start to swim. The flickering lights recede as the darkness envelops them and boney arms start to wrap around them, dragging them further into the darkness.

Friends Reunited

Francesca and Joe had met that September morning as they took their desks on the first day of secondary school. Within the hour, Joe's head had been fully turned by Francesca's upturned nose, long Crystal Tips hair, self-possession, and the German army jacket that smelt of wet dog when it rained. She, carefree and self-assured, toyed with the boy.

Her fancy lay elsewhere. Older, interesting, mobile men held her attention, he was the day time interest.

Their relationship was bumpy, semi platonic and tempestuous; the bulwark they both needed was Jenny, the friend and confidant to both. She seemed happy to play this role and helped soften their edges.

The three of them continued as friends until the occasion of the last falling out. It was a silly argument that no one bothered to fix. Worn out, the three of them needed a break.

Twenty five years later, Francesca's friend noticed Joe on the Reunited site. The internet was still quite new and the Reunited site hinted at the interconnected world to come. It was responsible for bringing long lost friends into each other's orbit, and class photos back to life. Thanks to the Reunited site, desultory dances in school canteens could no longer be avoided by the serial refuseniks. Like it or not, friends were reunited. Unthinkable today, it also had people's telephone numbers on it.

So it happened that on an unremarkable Tuesday in February, a remarkable thing happened. Francesca phoned Joe and a new old relationship began.

Around ten years had passed since that phone call; Francesca and Joe had rarely been apart. The magnetic poles that initially fascinated and repelled them, flipped, and a strong attraction drew them tightly together. More than just nostalgia, it had always been there. They were just too immature to see it.

The world had also moved on from the first dabblings in social media. The Reunited site was now a forgotten corner of the internet, the lumpen PCs and dialup connections needed to access it, were things of yore. Shiny screens and always-on-internet, the new normal. A social media giant had arisen and gobbled up all before it. So ubiquitous had it become that it felt like all human life was here, jostling for attention, alive in your pocket, 2.55

"Do you know who I miss?"

"Jenny?" said Francesca.

"Jenny? Christ yes. I wonder what she's doing now?"

"I did see her about twenty years ago. We met up for a pint. She seemed distracted, and actually got a bit annoyed with me. She said I talked too much."

"Well…"

"Shut up. Maybe I did. Anyway, I didn't hear from her again after that."

"See if you can find her."

"I wouldn't know where to start."

"Try with her name…"

The endless scroll of Jennies produced by the search, yielded nothing. It would have been easier if she'd had an unusual name, but Smith was going to be impossible.

Friends of friends? None gave any results

The immediate thought faded, and idle scrolling re-established its daily hold.

It remained that way until one day, while looking at the app, Francesca thinks she sees something in the background of a family photo, of someone she didn't really know. She pauses, dragging the timeline down toward her. The image has just left her screen, she retraces her virtual steps. Something in the app must have refreshed, because the photo has gone. Back and forth she goes. No such photo seems to exist.

What had caught her eye, in the background of a blurred snap, was the image of what looked very much like Jenny. Half hidden, slightly older, long hair tied elegantly from her face, but unmistakably, Jenny. She restarts the app and renews her search. Nothing. The hand holding her phone falls into her lap and she lifts her head.

The memory of Jenny came back, a female friend when she had none to speak of. Constant Jenny, she always seemed to pop up when needed. A car would appear on a Friday night and a door would fling open, a smiling face would shout "Get in!" and off they would hare, to lord knows where.

Joe had an entirely different memory of Jenny. To him Jenny was a friend indeed. His juvenile yearning for the impossible Francesca, had brought them a closeness. Joe and Jenny shared a nascent politics which railed against the prevailing heft. That and a love of break time cigarettes up the field, bound them in a temporal alliance.

Decades later, the suggestion from Francesca, they try to find Jenny, fell upon fertile ground. Warm memories of shared times would be great to revive, like the closing of a loop; they would sit and laugh about those days, sharing memories, only the three of them had, over a pint. It would be warm and wonderful.

Time passed. On a rainy day in June, Joe was looking through the infinite timeline that comprised his online life, when he thought he noticed something in the background of a blurry snap from someone else's life. This time though, he caught the image before it could disappear from the screen.

Dragging the picture back to the centre of the screen, he stabs at it. Pinching the image, he enlarges the face in the background. Could that be her? His own recollection of Jenny was idealised and hazy but he knew Francesca would know straight away.

Squeezing the sides of his phone, it flashed and a thumbnail of the image shrank to the bottom left hand side of his screen. Tapping it, he quickly cropped it and sent it to Francesca, with the label "Jenny?"

Ten seconds later the phone rang.

"Where did you see this?"

"It's from someone I don't know. I mean someone I do know, but is a friend of a friend, who's tagged into it, and she happens to be in the background. It is her, isn't it?"

"Yes it's her. Can't you look to see their friends, see if she's in there?"

"I can't. Everything's private. I'll try messaging my friend to see if he can help."

"Do it now!"

"I'm doing it. Get off the phone."

Francesca has gone. A message is prepared and sent. Nothing. A week passes, Francesca is insisting Joe follows it up. "Give them a chance, I've never even met them!" counters Joe.

Three days later, a notification arrives. Eagerly, Joe opens the message, reading it, his excitement is short lived. He messages Francesca. "They can't help. The person who's tagged them into the photo has blocked them, left social media and disappeared. It's a dead end I'm afraid.

Francesca slumps slightly at the news. "Can't we contact them somehow?"

"How? They're a friend of a friend of a friend who's blocked them, and left the internet. I wouldn't know where to start."

Reluctantly, they let the idea drop.

Months pass. Summer comes and goes. Jenny bubbles up in conversation, then returns to the hinterland of half-forgotten things.

A Sunday morning in November, the sun leans into low slung clouds, Francesca 's phone wolf whistles, a message has arrived.

Francesca isn't the sort to immediately respond to notifications; by contrast, Joe sees any red circles as an affront to the cleanliness of his Home Screen. For Joe, notifications are to be shot on sight. For Francesca notifications are just part of the ecosystem, invisible, stumbled upon whilst doing something else.

A week later, the message was noticed. An unknown number, she pauses and after a second she opens it. The message slides into view.

"Hi Francesca. J x"

Francesca stops. She's really not been expecting this. J? Jenny? Immediately she returns to the message, stabbing at the screen and calls the number. After a few seconds a screeching tone, then a voice: "The number you have called is not recognised, please try again. The number you have called is not recognised. Please try again…" The voice tails off as she lowers the phone from her ear.

That's fucking weird. She tries again. Same result. While Francesca is contemplating her next move, a sudden ping startles her. Same number, new message. Francesca 's thumb lingers over the red circle.

Tentatively, she depresses the image and another message slides into view.

"Wanna be friends? J x"

Just as Francesca lifts her thumb from the screen, a loud echoing 'ting' arrives. This isn't a message. Jumping to her Home Screen, she scans the apps, and there on her social app id the source of the alert. She opens it, and waiting for her is a new friend request.

Normally, this being from an old friend, she would have opened it, but the business with the messages and unknown numbers gave her cause to pause. This could be a scam.

She puts her phone down, rests her hands on her knees and steadies herself. She needs to talk to Joe, but he is out. So rather than pick up her phone to call him, she sits and waits, staring at the glossy slab of technology in front of her.

When she hears the key in the lock and Joe walks in, she calls for him from upstairs.

"Yes, one minute my love, I just need a pee."

A minute later, clomping footsteps round the corner and the black draped figure of Joe arrives, cold still clinging to his coat. He drops to the bed and sits next to Francesca.

"What is it my lovely?"

"This," she replies, showing him the first message.

"Oh wow, Jenny? Great! Did you call her?"

"Yes of course I did, but listen." She calls the number again, with the same result as before.

"Then this arrived."

"What? Another message? From the same number? That's a bit weird."

"Then I got this."

She moves a thumb across the screen in a well-practised arc and reveals the unopened friend request.

"Open it. Why haven't you opened it? It's from Jenny. It's what we've wanted. Open it."

Francesca shoots Joe a look, a look of trepidation. Her thumb hovers over the link.

"Here, give it here, I'll do it…"

Joe goes to grab Francesca's phone. She holds it out of reach.

"No, I'll do it." Hesitating for a fraction of a second, she firmly places her thumb on top of the notification. Releasing it, Jenny's profile pops into view.

"Let's have a decco before you accept, she might be a nutter now."

Francesca clicks the profile picture. The picture isn't of Jenny, instead there is a picture of a wood, with what looks like a passageway worn through the tangle of branches. She tried to go further into her profile

"Urgh, it's private."

"You'll have to accept her friend request then if you want to see some more."

Jenny's profile had no other info, no birthday, jobs, books liked, films seen or status, except for one detail. Her school. She had filled in the details of the school she'd attended.

"Lol. See it must be her. How many other Jenny's do we know who went to our school at the time we were there? It's her alright. Accept it "

Francesca, scrolls up and down a few times.

"What are you waiting for? Accept it. We can chat to her then."

Francesca's thumb hovers over the blue 'Confirm' button, until it involuntarily twitches its ascent, as if her thumb has decided for her. Francesca almost drops the phone in surprise. Her other hand rises to cradle it and they both stare at the screen.

Joe reaches over Francesca's shoulder and jabs at Jenny's picture. Her profile fills the screen. It is definitely Jenny alright. There she is, exactly as they both recalled. Images from another time, before smartphones and instant communication. There is Jenny in the pub, rollie in hand, three quarters of a pint of something dark and heady before her. Her long chestnut hair swept behind her ears, a broad smile on her lips, eyes looking directly at the camera.

"Is that the Riser? Looks like it."

Francesca presses the photo until it springs into its own window. Zooming in with thumb and forefinger, she pecks at the image, enlarging it until it is a blur. Releasing the image, it snaps back to its original size.

"Yeah that's the Riser. I remember the day. I think I took this picture."

"Wow. How weird after all this time. That's the first thing you see."

Joe's phone tings. He takes his phone from his pocket, and unlocks it with a glance. A new notification, a friend request from Jenny. Eagerly, he clicks the Confirm button.

Opening her profile, he too is greeted by an image of a long time past. Only this time there was no pub and smiling girl. It was him, from another lifetime. He recognises himself, almost despite the picture served up. In it, he is gaunt, his clothes, no more than rags really, hanging from his emaciated frame. A cigarette no thicker than a blade of grass, gripped between his boney fingers, pressed to pursed lips. He had one eye a squint, as if the smoke from the rollie had taken an unpleasant turn and caught him square on. He was leaning on the bonnet of a powder blue Triumph Herald.

"Let me see," Francesca grabs his phone. "God. Is that you? You look awful!"

She hands his phone back to him and returns to her own screen.

For a moment, they both silently tap and drag through the images on their phones.

"Do you notice anything odd about Jenny's profile?" Francesca askes Joe.

"She hasn't actually posted anything. These are all albums of photos."

They scroll back through the years.

"There's nothing on here that I don't remember. It looks like I was present at every single one of these pictures. Either I took it, or I'm in it. Where's the up-to-date stuff?"

"Well, there's only a few pics in her profile, and I'm in all of them. Are you sure we're looking at the same person?"

They hold their phones up side by side and something strange happens. Gone are the photos, replaced by a live stream that spans the two phones.

Joe sits back and Francesca turns to face him.

"What the fuck was that?"

"I don't know. I've never seen anything like it before!"

Joe looks at his phone. This time Jenny's profile is blank, save for the picture of the copse.

"Francesca, look at your phone. What's in Jenny's profile?"

"Fuck off! You look." Francesca fires back. Joe looks. He sees the same image of the wood.

"I see a wood. Now you look. What do you see?"

Francesca 's phone has locked itself. She gingerly lifts her eyes toward the screen. The padlock swings open.

"Open the app. Come on, let's see it."

Francesca pokes out a middle finger and slowly drags the screen up. Expanding into view is Jenny's profile. In it is the picture of the same wood.

Joe extends an arm toward Francesca 's phone. He places it next to Francesca's and the live stream resumes. They are both breathing heavily, their hands shake slightly. A woman in a soft mellifluous tone, is singing a song neither of them can quite recognise. It is night time, and a camera light illuminates the scene. Footsteps break twigs under foot as the transmission continues.

Francesca and Joe are transfixed. Instinctively they reach for each other's hands.

The stream goes on. They catch a glimpse of a part of the person holding the camera. A wisp of chestnut hair and a brief puff of smoke partially obscure the lens, as the streamer heads further into the thicket.

Francesca and Joe squeeze each other's hands tighter.

Suddenly, the streamer stops. There is a pause; the camera slowly turns around.

"Hello you two. I'm so glad you've decided to be my friends."

Francesca and Joe let out an involuntary gasp, "Jenny?"

It is Jenny. There she stands before them. The camera appears to have fixed its position in space. Jenny takes a step backwards so they can see all of her. She walks slowly from one phone screen to another whilst looking directly into the camera. Wearing a white slip, more like a night shirt, she holds a cigarette in the fingers of her left hand, and runs the other through her hair, wrapping her long tresses behind one ear.

"Jenny?" Francesca leans forward and squints at the image, she goes to reach out to pinch the screen, hoping to enlarge the picture but stops short as Jenny begins to speak.

"Well, it's been a long time since we three met." She allows herself a half smile at her joke.

"All these years I've been waiting. Waiting for this moment, and now it's here. The glorious moment. I'm going to try to savour it. Such a long time I've been waiting."

Francesca has too many questions, and they tumble out one after another. "Where are you? Where have you been? Why couldn't we find you? Jenny, what's going on?"

Jenny casts a glance at Joe.

"Hello Joe. Still smoking?"

"No. No Jenny, I gave up years ago. What's going on? Where are you?"

"Can't you see? I'm in the woods. In the trees. I've been here for so long. It's so lonely here. I've been waiting for my friends to come and see me. Not just any friends but my special, chalk and cheese friends. The only friends who can help me. The only ones I need."

Francesca watches, as Jenny skips between the screens, her mood has lifted and she seems positively happy now.

"I still don't understand. How can we help you, and why does it have to be us? You've always had lots of friends. Obviously better friends, as we've not seen you for over twenty years. What can we do that they can't"

Jenny throws back her head and gives an uncontrolled laugh. Neither Francesca or Joe had ever seen her laugh like this before

"What can you do for me? What can you do for me?" She laughs again, "Why you've already done it!" She laughs harder and starts dancing and twirling between the screens.

"Here I've been for years. Trapped in this bleak wood with only the things of the night for company. They are not nice things. They come for you in the dark and finger your spine while you sleep. You can feel them licking at your ear while you wash. There's no sunlight here, just murk and darkness. Their putrid breath hangs in the air, and boney fingers tear at your clothing day and night."

Jenny rushes toward the camera, her face filling both screens. "There is no respite, everyday the same, never seeing them, they're always there, testing, teasing, biting."

Francesca and Joe recoil. Francesca turns to Joe. "Is this real?"

Joe addresses the screen, "What the fuck has this got to do with us?"

Jenny steps back. "Very little to be honest and that is the best bit. You're completely blameless. The only thing you've done wrong is accept my friend request! I needed you to invite me in, and now you have, the damage is done!" She laughs again and reaches out a hand

"Turn the fucking thing off!" Francesca yells at Joe.

Joe tries to separate the phones but they're stuck together. He's holding both phones and is desperately searching for the off button, when from the screen, a hand reaches out and grabs his wrist.

Joe lets out a yelp of pain as the grip tightens. Francesca starts pinching and clawing at the hand but then another shoots through and grabs her. Jenny is so strong, she yanks and wrenches at their hands, bit by bit pulling them toward the screen, laughing and taunting them as she reels them in.

"Two for one, two for one!"

Francesca and Joe's faces are side by side on the threshold of the screen now. They're both screaming and imploring Jenny to stop. But she won't stop and redoubles her efforts, she hauls and drags at them until they are both pulled through the glass, on to the other side, and into the wood 23.25

On landing they lie in the leaf litter trying to catch their breath. Jenny stands above them. She looks upon the pathetic figures they have become, and gives Joe a kick for good measure.

"Well, here you are my friends. In my place now. We shall not meet again. I suppose I should thank you. She laughs for a final time and does a low courtesy, before jumping up into the small rectangle of light from which they came.

Francesca gets to her feet and runs toward the light. "No Jenny, don't leave us here. Why would you do this?"

"Your turn!" Jenny calls back.

Joe feels something touch his neck and calls out "Jenny!"

On the other side of the screen, Jenny is in their bedroom. Holding their phones. Just one last thing to do. She opens her account and searches for Francesca and Joe.

She unfriends them both.

"And block!"

Locking the phones, she tosses them on the bed, switches off the light and leaves the room.

Nightmare

As children we all have nightmares, especially when we're ill.

This. Is mine

I'm hot. So hot. My head is burning. But the room is so cold. Snow falls on The sore blanket I avoid touching. Wrapping the bri-nylon around its corners I fight the cold

Tonsils raging. Nostrils blocked. Mouth Dry. Painful. I dare not cough. My chest raw. I arch and stretch. Again and again.

Can't swallow. Razors. Hearing hurts. My skin as sore as the rough blanket that covers me. Diarrhoea. Thick brown piss. Hawked up phlegm cathedrals.

Shaky limbs. Head not my own.

Seventies ill. Yellow penicillin. Linctus. Lucozade. Vick mumps. On one side. On one side.

Why are you here?

I can't get home

It's too far

Come down here.

I can't move

Come. I can hear it

I can't move

Come quickly

My feet won't move

Over here

It's coming

Breath out of breath

Move.

I'm hot. Sweating. I'm too hot

It's me

What?

It's me.

But you're…

Look at me

I can't see your face

Give me your hands

Touch my face

I can't see

Your face, it feels wrong. Don't cry. I didn't mean it

Come. Run

I'm trying. Why am I so heavy. I can see you. I can't get close.

Atom bombs?

I must get home. It's far away. There's nothing left. A wasteland. Broken. Burning. The pall of death everywhere

So many corners. Chess board floors. Big rooms. So many big rooms. This is a big house

Impossible rocks

Why is it so cold? I'm soaking. Wet through. My bedroom is bleeding.

I'm bleeding. My nose. The pillow. Torn sheets. Tangled. Rough blanket. Vick.

The light under the door. The whistle in my ears

Dry. I'm so dry.

Burning.

Hot.

Gone

Gone

Gone

Gone

Gone.

Mill Hill

"I love it up here. You can see five different modes of transport you know."

"What? Five? Ok then I'll bite. Road, rail, sea and what are the other two"

"Air."

"Air? Oh yeah, I'd not realised that before, but you're right. I don't really think of the airport as an airport."

"Well, it's got planes taking off from it, and it's over there." Gerry, points to the small municipal airfield just beyond the river.

"And the fifth?"

"Horses."

"Where?"

"There, in the field, under the flyover."

It takes Fliss a second to locate them. "Ok you win."

"It's really stunning up here, the way the land opens out into the valley. Even the road looks like it belongs here, and to cap it all you have the Downs. They are so beautiful."

Fliss and Gerry stand on the edge of the hill which overlooks the river valley that forms this part of Sussex.

A crisp wind whips up the side of the hill so briskly, that for many years this was a popular site for hang gliders.

Over time, the increasing death toll of young long-haired men, had forced the site to be closed to them.

They both plunge their hands deep into their pockets. It's cold and the chill makes them wince.

"C'mon, let's go for a wander"

Turning, they head toward the copse behind them.

The local council had spent quite a bit of money making the site accessible. Dark gravel paths were laid through the thicket. Something to do with the millennium, so the signs said.

They unhitch the gate and step into the wood.

"Remember the country code!"

"Remember! How can I forget? They showed us so many public information films through the seventies, I'm never going to forget to shut the gate."

"Or not to fly a kite near pylons!"

They both laugh.

Out of the wind the temperature rises a few degrees, just enough to warrant the loosening of a scarf a little.

The copse is very old and not managed in the traditional way. Only minimal human intervention is required. The wind selects the trees it wishes to prune. The remainder cling to the thin, chalky topsoil, unable to get a decent footing. The wood has been on the side of this hill for hundreds, if not thousands of years, however the trees are no more than 50 or 60 years old at most. Except, that is, for one.

This ancient oak stands in the middle of the wood. It is not at all tall. The crown lost to the wind as it grew. Denied upward growth, its boughs spread outwards. From its dark, squat trunk, around ten feet up, four sturdy branches protrude at right angles to each other. They have an odd uniformity about them. A few smaller branches at the ends, hold the scant summer foliage, now absent.

They both look up at it.

"If only trees could talk, eh?"

"We can talk to them," Gerry says.

"Yes, but have we got anything to say they want to hear?"

They both chuckle again, and resume their walk. Turning a corner on the edge of the trees, they encounter a new view. On rolling downland, sheep, and cattle graze in large neat fields. There is so much space up here, you can see the shadows of clouds, skittering across field after field.

"Can you imagine what it must have been like living up here before electricity and running water Fliss? How cold it must have been tending livestock in the wind and rain? Imagine being a peasant farmer clinging to the side of this hill."

"Even if you had shelter, you wouldn't have proper windows, the drafts! Oh my god, I remember what the drafts were like when I was a girl. They'd whistle around your ankles. None of the windows fitted properly and there was a gap under every door you could get your fist in. Did no one think draft excluders were a good idea?"

"We had one, just the one mind, in the shape of a sausage dog. It went up against the kitchen door for some reason, exactly where it was least effective. People just seemed to put up with it in those days. I remember when our house got central heating. All the floors came up, it took weeks to put in."

"Did it make a difference?"

"No, not really, the drafts saw to that."

They share a wistful smile at the memory.

60

Turning away, they head back into the wood.

"Look someone has made a den."

A few sticks have been piled up to form a rudimentary shelter.

"Why is it that every single wood I've ever been in has one of these?"

They go over and examine it.

"I think it might have something to do with the Scouts."

"Does it?"

"No idea."

Gerry rolls his eyes.

"I didn't think the wood was quite this big, we seem to have been walking for a long while now. I'm starting to get cold. Can you see the car park?"

"No. I can only see a path over there." Fliss points to a muddy track that seems strangely out of place, considering all the effort the council has gone to, to make the wood accessible.

"Looks a bit muddy."

"If we stick to the edges, it shouldn't be too bad. I think it's heading out. Once we're out we can get our bearings. There's no point trying while we're still in here."

"Agreed."

They straddle the path, managing to miss most of the mud. Soon they are out of the wood.

"Right where are we?" They look at their phones.

"I've got no coverage at all. You?"

"Nope, no bars. Look." Gerry holds his phone up for inspection.

"You'd think you'd get something up here. Truly Hill isn't far away and there's a transmitter on top of it!"

"Nope, nothing."

Just then, a little way off, a person comes around the corner.

"Look there's someone, we can ask them if they know."

"Good idea, let's go."

They set off toward the figure. As they get closer, they notice something about his clothes. They are drab, and rough looking, they clearly haven't seen the inside of a washing machine in years, or ever. He is not wearing shoes as such. They look more like sandals. About his ankles are laced cloths which partially cover the footwear.

"What's he dressed like?"

"He looks like a 15th century peasant. They must have a re-enactment society around here or something."

"Hey, hello!" They wave at him. He stops.

Gerry raises his voice a little, "Hey can you tell us the way back to the car park? We've got a bit lost."

The figure turns and scampers off back around the corner.

"Bit rude."

"It certainly was, let's follow him, I'm sure there will be others."

The two of them head in his direction. They round the corner and they see what appears to be a small mediaeval encampment.

"Blimey. I didn't expect to see that!"

"It's very realistic."

Before them, is a village populated with pigs and sheep in pens. A cow is wandering through the scene. It is being driven by what looks like a girl of no more than 10.

They stroll up to her, "Hey little girl, this village is very realistic. What detail!" The girl looks askance at them and moves the cow on with her stick.

"Where are your parents? We need some directions."

The girl glances over her shoulder to one of the shacks dotted around a central smouldering fire.

"Right, thank you."

They take a few paces on and Gerry whispers to Fliss, "She's bloody odd too. They're really taking this seriously, aren't they?"

"Too bloody seriously. Let's get the directions and get out of here."

They approach the shack.

"Where do I knock? There's no door, just a cloth."

"I don't know. Improvise."

Fliss coughs loudly. "Excuse me? Can you tell us where the car park is? I'm afraid we've got a little lost"

From inside the hut, they can hear a rustling. Some coughing and muttering follows. Soon after, a head pops out. It looks them up and down.

"Hwone ú?"

"I'm sorry, I didn't catch that."

"It sounded like French? Maybe they're French."

"French? Why would they be camped up here, and even if they were they didn't build all this. Let me try."

"Ou et la car park?"

The hut dweller pushes through the cloth door and stands in front of them. He can't be more than 5'2, his hair is matted and it doesn't look like he's ever had a bath. He also smells like a goat.

They both take half a step back as the smell is quite overpowering. Soon more heads appear. Before long there is a crowd of villagers surrounding them. A vigorous discussion is underway, centring, it seems, on the intruders.

"Can you catch any of it?" Hisses Fliss.

"Not a word. The more I listen to it, the less like French it sounds. There's the odd word but it sounds more like old English."

"Old English? Now there's commitment to role play!"

Gerry elbows Fliss and they both enjoy the comment.

"Wh'rehas't thee cometh from?"

"Oh, I see very good. We comest from Londinium, can you-estshowest us to ye old-e woldey car park-e please-eth."

"I say, don't take the piss Fliss, we'll never get out of here."

The villagers talk animatedly amongst themselves for a while.

Gerry reaches into his pocket for his phone. Pulling it out, he looks at the screen. "Nope, still no signal"

The villagers abruptly stop talking. They've spotted the phone. Suddenly the mood darkens.

There's a kerfuffle from near the back of the crowd and the children suddenly disappear.

"Fuck, Gerry, what have you done?"

"I'm not sure. Leave it to me, I can sort this out in a second."

"Look, we're really sorry to have disturbed you. We just want to get back in our car and go home. Can you help us or not?"

What appears to be the leader of the village produces a dagger from his belt, and advances on them. He presses it to Gerry's throat and beckons with his hand to give him the phone.

"Fuck, I'm being robbed. Fliss do something!"

But Fliss can't do anything. The villagers have got her by the arms and they are holding her prisoner.

"This escalated really fucking quickly, how the fuck do we get out of here?"

The villagers go through their pockets and find Fliss's phone and her car keys.

The tribe prod them with their pikes, and daggers, pushing them into one of the empty pig pens. The crowd withdraws, and several men are left behind to guard the scared and confused travellers.

An angry exchange of views follows, as their keys and phones are examined carefully by what look like the village elders. After about an hour of this, the row abates and the council seems to come to some sort of conclusion.

The village chief approaches the makeshift gaol.

"We has't hath decided. Thou art hags. And th're's only one thing we doth with hags.

To the tree." With a flourish he motions in the direction of the wood.

"To the tree? To the tree? What the fuck does that mean?" Gerry rasps.

"I don't fucking know but it doesn't sound fucking brilliant does it Gerry?"

"Look Fliss, we can't stay here, when they open the gate, I'm going to rush them, see if you can escape. I'm a good head taller than them. I should be able to take them on."

"Fucking hell Gerry, this isn't what I expected when I said let's go for a walk. If we get out of this, I'll never say it again."

Half a dozen of the bigger men advance on the pen, as the gate opens, Gerry punches the chief as hard as he can, and shouts,

"Run Fliss, run!"

Fliss starts to run but is tripped up by some of the women. They pounce on her prone body and begin to bind her hands and feet. She calls out, "Gerry!"

But there's nothing he can do. A few of them have jumped on him and they have dragged him to the ground. They are tightly tying him up. His struggling isn't helping, only making it worse for him.

Once they both have been incapacitated, they are dumped, face down, side by side on the ground, while the villagers prepare for what comes next.

"How the fuck did we get here? Who are these fucking hillbillies. Do they think we won't be missed?"

"We might not be."

"What?"

"We might not be. I've read about this. It's a time slip. We've stumbled through a doorway, back in time. It must have been when we stepped off the path to look at that tree. I think we may be fucked."

"Have you lost your fucking mind Fliss? Are you seriously saying…"

"Well, yes, look where we are."

They look up from the ground. The villagers don't look like they're acting. The children reappear and run toward them. A pack of barking dogs snap at the two of them, as the laughing children poke them with sharp sticks.

The adults come over to Gerry and Fliss, lifting them up, they drag them toward the old oak tree at the centre of the copse.

"Fuck. Fuck. Fuck."

"Are we going to die Gerry?"

"Ah fuck, fucking hell. Fuck."

The chief takes a coiled rope from a basket they've brought with them and throws it over one of the branches of the ancient tree. He ties one end to a smaller branch and then repeats the process with another rope on another bough. The women and children drag a long bench from the village and put it under the tree. The chief climbs on it and starts to tie a noose on the free end of the rope. He repeats the process with the other rope.

"Fucking hell! They're going to hang us!"

"You're fucking kidding. Because of the phone?"

"They think we're witches."

"Witches? I don't believe this. You people are fucking insane!"

The villagers haul them to their feet and stand them on the bench. The Chief slips the noose over their heads.

Gerry starts to beg for their lives.

"Please stop. We're not witches we're…"

The Chief kicks the bench out from under their feet. The villagers give a loud cheer, and clap as the strangers start their dance of death, at the end of the rope.

Stone Tape Theory

It is early afternoon when Ed Brackenbury disembarks at Scotscalder Station. To say the station is remote is a gross understatement.

Even for the Scottish Highlands, the tiny, seldom-used station is isolated. It's on the mainland, but only just.

Ed watches the train trundle off into the distance as he stands on the platform beside his small suitcase. The luggage says a lot about Ed. It is old fashioned and a bit battered. A striped cloth belt keeps the contents inside, and it's heavier than it needs to be. Picking it up he turns and heads for the exit.

Outside the station sits a single Taxi. The driver is leaning on the bonnet, smoking.

"Afternoon. Where you going?"

"Good afternoon. I'm going to Ben Dorray."

"Ben Dorray eh? Are you to do with the radio? There's not much else up there."

"Well, yes, sort of. Will you take me there?"

"Aye. Get in."

The driver takes the case from Ed and puts it in the boot of the car. Ed gets in the back. .

"How far is it?"

"Not far. Well, not in miles, but in other ways it's a long way off. Where are you staying?"

Ed reaches into his pocket and pulls out a rumpled piece of paper, and hands it to the driver.

The driver glances at the address and passes it back to his passenger. "Oh. You're staying there are you?"

"Is there a problem?" Ed asks

"No. No problem." The driver starts the engine, checks his mirrors and heads for the tower..

The Ben Dorray transmitter is the only radio mast for miles and miles. Its position on the top of the mull, means that it has a reach that far outweighs its size. On a good day the signal can be picked up in the Faroe Islands.

Usually, the transmitter simply relays local community radio stations, who share the available airtime between themselves. The output is steady, worthy, and a bit boring, but it provides a lifeline to the isolated highland communities that would otherwise have to rely on crackly shortwave radio for their news and entertainment.

Thirty minutes later, the taxi pulls up at the transmitter. Next to it is a portacabin. It's grubby and the windows are barred. A small ramp with a wobbly handrail leads up to the entrance.

"Would you mind waiting?" Ed asks the driver. "I want to be sure I can get in."

"Aye. I'll wait." The driver turns off the engine, leans out of the window and lights another cigarette.

Ed fishes for the keys in his pocket. He sifts through the bundle until he finds the one with BD-A written on it in grubby Tippex. He approaches the Portacabin and tries the key in the door.

It's very stiff. It barely moves when he tries to turn it, he's a little concerned about breaking the key off in the lock.

Abruptly, the driver appears behind him and shakes a can of WD40 next to his ear.

"Hear you go Sonny. There's a lot of weather up here. We're always doing this, He waves the red plastic straw at the lock and gives it a couple of firm squirts.

Some of the liquid hits Ed's hand, and runs down his arm. The smell is distinctively strong. He reaches into his pocket, pulls out a tissue, and wipes the fluid from his arm.

Gradually the lock begins to move. The driver gives it another long squirt, and turns the key vigorously back and forth until, with a click, the door opens.

"There. That'll give you nae more trouble while you're here."

"Thank you." Ed replies awkwardly. Squeezing past the driver, he enters the cabin.

"I'll be off now then will I?" The driver hovers by the door.

"What? Oh yes. I'm sorry." Ed pays the driver the fare and gives him a tip.

"Thank you for waiting, and helping with the door. Do you have a card? I'm going to need collecting in a day or two."

The driver fishes around in his jacket pocket and produces a crumpled card. He straightens it out as best he can. It is covered in what smells like engine oil and is badly creased.

"Here you go." The driver hands the oily card to Ed.

"Leave a message if I'm not there, and I'll come and get you."

"Thank you." Ed mumbles.

Ed looks at the brown Bakelite phone on the desk. The body is chipped and the dial is starting to rust. "I'll call you on that."

"You sure it still works?"

Ed picks up the handset and holds it to his ear. He can hear the dial tone. "Yes it sounds like it." He blows into the mouthpiece. "Yes, I can hear myself, so I'm going to say this is working."

"On your head be it." The driver deadpans as he leaves.

Ed closes the door. The wind is really getting up now, and it's starting to get dark.

He takes another piece of paper from his pocket and reads the instructions. Making his way to the desk, he sits behind it, and feels for the top drawer in front of him. He pulls it open with both hands and looks inside.

The drawer is empty save for another key. A cruddy string attaches a dog-eared paper tag to the key. On it, the single word 'Cabin' is scrawled in spidery red ink.

Ed takes the key from the drawer and leaves the portacabin. At the threshold, he tries the key in the door a few times, just to be sure he can open it again. Once satisfied that he can re-enter, he pulls the door to, and locks it behind him.

He traverses the short distance to the old stone bothy, that will be his home for the next few days.

Ed now finds himself alone in the Scottish Highlands, following a curious set of coincidences that began six months earlier.

By trade Ed is a sound technician. He had always been fascinated by sound. The greatest gift he received as a child was the solid Sony portable TC-92 cassette tape 'Corder', as it was awkwardly named, that he got for his ninth birthday. His favourite part of it was the big red 'Record' button.

Pushing this button was like opening a portal to another universe. It was a place Ed visited frequently.

His obsession with sound had meant that he'd got very good at working with it. So good in fact, that as an adult he found himself working on the studio sessions for some of the biggest artists of the day.

What these huge stars, or rather the 'Suits' that paid his wages, liked about working with Ed, was that he was so straight. He would always be on time for work, he was never drunk, high on drugs or unreliable. When you hired Ed, you got work done.

It was on one of these jobs, during some down time, that Ed made a rare foray into the daylight. The studio was very hot and thick with smoke from about a hundred joints, and he needed some air.

He opened the back door to the studio, and wedged it open with the crate that was kept solely for this purpose.

He stretched his arms and was about to sit down, when a loud "Careful man" came from behind him.

There sitting on the low wall behind the door, was a wizened old man, clutching what was clearly a small joint between his yellowing fingers.

"Oh sorry, I didn't see you there."

"No worries, hombre. I was sort of hiding anyways". The man spoke in a soft brogue that seemed quite at odds with his appearance.

Ed hesitated for a moment, before asking "Why are you hiding?"

"I'm their roadie." He waves his thumb over his shoulder, back toward the studio.

"They're all so minced now, if they see me, they'll just want me to go and get more drugs, and to be honest, I'm getting a bit too old for all of this, so I'll just hide here until they pass out."

"Fair enough. It won't be long the way they're going. I don't see the fun in it myself. They're paying a lot to be in there, and as far as I can hear, 95% of what they're recording is incoherent noise. I'm glad I'm not paying for it is all I can say. I don't know why they all come here to be honest, there's just too many distractions."

The old man takes another big lug on his spliff. "That reminds me of a tale I heard a while back."

"Oh yes?" Ed's not really listening, he glances at his watch.

"Yeah. It's an odd one."

Ed's ears prick up slightly at this.

"What do you mean?" Ed, for all his straightness, loves a good mystery, and while he doesn't one hundred percent buy into all of the odd stories he'd heard over the years, especially from musicians and assorted hangers on, he was still interested to hear them.

"Well I'm not sure I should tell you. It's such a weird story, I don't know if I believe it or not."

"Go on, I'm all ears."

"Ok then, but don't blame me if it gives you nightmares."

He wags a skeletal finger at him.

Ed stifles a laugh, like he's going to be worried about this old stoner's fever dreams.

The veteran stage hand repeatedly flicks at his lighter until it sparks into life. The joint is rotated in the flame 'till it's fully alight. The roadie takes a drag, and blows a plume of pungent smoke over in Ed's direction.

"Well this is what I heard, like I said, I don't know if it's true, but it still gives me the creeps..."

"Around ten years ago, a local band decided, like you said, that there were just too many distractions in the city. They needed to finish their second album. The first had been a big hit, but they were struggling with the difficult second album. A cliche I know, but it happens to be true a lot of the time, if you think about it."

"A first album might have taken years to write. Adding songs over time, perfecting them, honing them, shaping an album. It gets released, everyone loves it! They tour it for a couple of years. Everyone's happy."

"Then it comes time to do the second album, but you've got no songs left. You might have a few half ideas, but you quickly find you're two and a half years in, and you've suddenly got to produce an album out of thin air, and it's got to be at least as good as the first one you spent years perfecting. It's no wonder some of them struggle."

"Anyway, they weren't getting anywhere down here, so the lead singer hears about this really isolated place in Scotland, that's got a small radio transmitter and an old stone bothy next to it. Immediately he thinks that this is the solution to their problems, and persuades the other band members that this is going to be the perfect place to finish the album…"

It's ten years earlier and the band are sitting on the low wall outside the same studio. They are all smoking. It's the beginning of Autumn. The sun is bright and just starting to lose its heat in the day, but it's not quite cold enough to drive them inside while they smoke.

"Really? What about Montserrat, I hear that's really nice at this time of year?"

"Dude, the highlands of Scotland, in September? I vote Montserrat"

"Yeah, me too." The drummer chips in.

"Band meeting!" The singer arrives, late as ever.

"What,? We're having it."

"Not without me you're not."

"Come on then, what is it?"

"Scotland…" He begins

The others give a collective groan.

"Hear me out. I'd love to go to the Caribbean to finish the record, but I'm pretty sure that all we would end up doing is even more booze and drugs."

"We'd be no closer to finishing the record than we would if we stayed here. Plus, we'd have spent all the money we made from the first album. We'll go to Montserrat for the next one. I promise."

The band looked at each other. They knew that once he'd made his mind up there really wasn't much point in arguing further. He'd just threaten to leave, like he does every time he can't get his own way. They'd all end up giving in anyway, so why bother with the bother.

One day they'd call his bluff, but that day wasn't today, besides he was essentially correct. They all knew it. A reluctant message was sent to their manager, for him to arrange it.

Within the week, they were all on a train, heading north.

"What about the kit?"

"Robbo's arranged for it to be sent ahead. He's hired a portable mixing desk and the studio is being set up now. It should all be waiting for us."

"How much is all that costing?" Asks the bass player.

"Less than one ticket to Montserrat!" The singer pings back.

"Where are we going to sleep? I've seen a picture of the place, it's tiny, even without all the gear in there. It won't fit us all in."

"Don't worry, there's a couple of caravans. We'll have to share, but that should just give us more reason to finish the album, so we can get back to civilization even quicker."

No one liked the sound of this. They hadn't shared rooms for a couple of years, and weren't keen to go back to it, but then again he was right. Anything to get the fucking record finished.

When they arrived at the station, the taxi had to make two trips to get them to their makeshift recording studio. It was literally in the middle of nowhere.

"Fucking hell, who thought this was a good idea?"

The five of them stood outside the bothy, looking like they'd just been beamed in from outer space. There were the four members of the band, and the sound engineer.

They left the producer in London. He was a dick, and they'd decided to try to produce the last few tracks themselves. If they fucked it up, then at least they'd have the tapes that they could play around with when they got back home.

The next day, after a damp, cold, uncomfortable night, the five of them coughed, spluttered, and shuffled into the studio.

The 'studio' was a single room. Its damp walls were hung with thick blackout curtains and an old heavy woollen rug covered the floor. Somehow a portable mixing desk had been squeezed in through the old narrow door. Cables and stands of various uses were laid out. The drums were placed in a rickety booth that looked like it was just about to fall over. A generator positioned some way away outside, supplied the power the local grid was incapable of providing.

The sound guy lit the wood burner in the corner of the room and they all huddled around it, nursing tepid tea, trying to warm up.

"I'm not so sure this was such a good idea, I'm fucking freezing and it's so damp. I don't feel very rock, or roll"

"Come on man, where's your sense of adventure?" The drummer parked himself on his drum stool, picked up his sticks and started playing. He was soon joined by the bass player and guitarist as they began to jam out the tune they had been struggling with for a few weeks now.

Gradually, they started to sound like a band, rather than four people with instruments they couldn't work out how to play.

The engineer clapped his headphones tightly to his ears, as if struggling to hear something.

The others noticed and stopped playing.

"What's up?"

"I don't know. There's a lot of noise in the room…"

"I wouldn't say it was that bad…"

"Shut up Sammy. Idiot."

"Obviously not that sort of noise. There's something in the background, I'm struggling to hear it."

'Is it the genny?"

"No, it's not that. It sounds like it's coming from within the room.'"

The guitarist chips in, "Play it back."

The engineer rewinds the tape and plays it over the monitors.

Under the sound of the band you can just about hear a murmuring. It's incredibly indistinct and could easily just be tape noise.

"Can you hear that? The engineer is very sure he can hear something.

Sound engineers are trained to hear noises that others usually miss, it's an important part of their job, to spot these sounds and eliminate them from recordings.

"Yeah, a bit. Does it matter?" Asks the drummer.

The engineer lifts his eyes from the mixing desk and glares at the drummer.

"No, none of it matters. In fact, why am I even here? I seem to be wasting my fucking time stuck up here, in the middle of fucking nowhere with a bunch of talentless cloth-eared losers. I might as well just leave the tape running and fuck off back to London right now!"

"Sorry dude… I didn't mean to…"

"Fucking amateurs. Tell me why am I even bothering..? Stupid me, these sessions just engineer themselves don't they? Well go on then, off you go…"

And with that, he flicks the tape machine on to record, picks up his coat and fags, and leaves the room slamming the door behind him.

"Fuck sake Dave, why did you have to go and say that? You know how fucking temperamental he is."

Brian, lays down his guitar and pulls on his coat. "I'll go and get him. I suggest we all take a break."

The remaining members look at each other and decide now would be a good time to look for some food. They head back to the caravans and see if there's anything for lunch.

Around an hour and a half later. The engineer has been persuaded to return, They've all had some food, which has helped lower the temperature in the room.

"Did no one switch this off?"

"What?"

"The tape, it's been rolling the whole time."

"Just rewind it dude. Keep the first bit from the morning though, that was getting somewhere" They all nod in agreement.

The engineer rewinds the tape. After several attempts he gets to the point in the tape where they decide to have lunch and they can hear themselves leaving the room.

He's just about to stop it, when a voice comes from the speaker. They all immediately stop what they're doing and look at the engineer.

"What the fuck was that?"

Then there's another voice. It sounds like it's answering the first voice.

They all get to their feet.

"What the fuck is going on? Who else is here?"

"No one is here. It's just us, there's no one around for miles."

"Then who the fuck is that talking?"

There's no doubt now. There is definitely someone talking on the tape.

"What are they saying? I can't make it out "

The taped conversation continues.

"This is fucking spooky. You lot better not be pissing us around."

"I'm not. I promise. I haven't even been here, have I?"

"That sounds like Gaelic?"

"Gaelic? Who the fuck speaks that anymore."

"Well not many, but they used to. When this was built, I bet they did."

The engineer stops the tape.

He lights a cigarette. "I didn't think this could be real."

He has their full attention.

"There's an idea that sounds can be captured by their surroundings. Like a tape recorder stores sounds by using magnets to arrange iron oxide particles on a tape. But instead of the tape, the sound gets saved in an object. Stone Tape Theory, yes that's what it's called."

"Are you being serious? Are you saying the tape recorded the playback from this building?"

"Why not? There's lots of iron ore around here. This building could easily contain iron particles. Why couldn't ancient shields or swords have become magnetised? Wave them about in the middle of an argument and bingo! You've got yourself a house sized tape recorder."

"We used to talk about it in college, but it was only ever one of those things we'd talk about when we'd dropped acid. I didn't think for a second it might actually be real"

"Play some more of the tape," the drummer says.

"Not for me. I'm out. This sort of thing really gets to me so I'm gone. Let me know when you're done" The guitarist picks up his things and leaves the room.

Once he's gone, the engineer pushes play on the tape. The background talking carries on. Then it goes quiet. They all lean in, straining to hear. Suddenly there is a loud crash and the tape breaks, lashing around and around on its spool.

"Fuck sake, that nearly gave me a heart attack. Was that on the tape?"

"I don't think so, it sounded like it came from upstairs."

They all look up.

"The problem with that,.." The drummer starts, "is there isn't an upstairs."

"Fuck me. It's all getting a bit Scooby-Doo. It must have come from outside then."

The singer heads for the door.

When he gets outside, there on the ground is a guitar. It's been smashed to pieces.

There is no sign of its owner.

From behind him, inside the bothy, comes the noise of loud cries and screams.

Rushing back in, he finds an empty room.

The instruments are scattered across the floor, and the curtains have been pulled from the walls. The only sign they'd been there recently, is the tape player, it's still running. The tape seemingly repaired. It is playing out the sounds of a group of people eating…

The old Roadie takes another long toke on his joint.

"The singer made it back to London. He was never the same again after that. They couldn't find a trace of the others, all that was left was their equipment"

"What about the tape? Where's that?"

"Well after the police had finished with it, they returned it to the singer as it was his property. Not sure after that. He went mad and ended up living in a dustbin in the Eastend somewhere. He died recently. It was a tragic end to what should have been a great career."

A couple of weeks after the Roadies tale, Ed noticed a small advert in the back of one of the trade newspapers for an engineer to go and work on some transmitters in the Highlands of Scotland.

"That's a coincidence," he thought. Included on the list was the Ben Dorry Station.

Something made him pick up the phone and arrange an interview.

Being the only suitable applicant, he'd got the job, and now found himself sitting in the exact same bothy as the one he'd heard in the old man's story.

It now boasted a bed and a small kitchen. The inside wasn't much warmer than the outside, so he lit the wood burner in the corner of the room.

Whilst not a superstitious man, he nonetheless felt slightly anxious about being in the room where three fully grown men had vanished all those years ago.

Sitting in silence, all he could hear was the sound of the rising gale curling around the stone walls. Occasionally the wood burner would surge with the wind, and it would give a small pop or crackle from the rough wood ablaze in it.

Picking up his suitcase, he placed it on the small table that stood in the middle of the room. Loosening the belt that held it together, he slipped it off and fiddled with the lock.

Eventually, it sprang open and he lifted the lid.

Amongst the few clothes and personal possessions he'd packed, was his old tape recorder.

Carefully lifting it out, he put it on the table and looked at it.

Was he really going to do this?

Whilst back in London, after he'd got the job, he started to do some research about the area.

In the 17th century there had been a spate of attacks on locals. It turned out there was a clan, much like Sawney Bean's further south, who had taken to cannibalism to supplement their starvation diet.

The war between the clans and the Redcoats had been raging for 40 years at that point, and the English would use famine as a weapon in the war of attrition between the Scots and themselves.

To begin with, the local clan turned to consuming human flesh out of necessity, as they were literally starving to death. The English had them pinned into a rugged and barren corner of the highlands.

Eating the soldiers they caught eventually became a way of taking some power back from the brutal invaders. However, the more they did it, the more they came to enjoy it. Soon, it was their preferred meat.

Could this be what the band had heard on the tapes?

It didn't explain their disappearance, but if he could prove that Stone Tape Theory was a real phenomena, he'd get some credit for something other than just being a sound engineer. A discovery that would ensure his name would forever be linked with the phenomena. He'd be in the sort of audio textbooks he liked to paw over in his spare time. Brackenbury's phenomena. Yeah, he liked the sound of that.

He picked up the suitcase and put it on the floor. Clearing the table he took the tape recorder and placed it as near to the middle as he could without measuring it.

Hesitating for an instant, he took two fingers and held them over the record and play buttons. Affirming to himself that this really was a good idea, he simultaneously firmly pressed both the keys down until the right hand cassette spool took up the slack and slowly started turning. He took a few steps backwards. Finding his keys he left the room, locking the door behind him.

.....

Two hours later, the sound of a key in the lock heralded his arrival back at the bothy, and the front door swung open.

Ed made straight for the bedside table. The tape had come to an end, the buttons sitting neatly in a row.

Leaning against the table, he picked up the tape recorder and pressed the rewind button.

Slowly at first, the tape started to turn. It gathered speed as the thin ribbon spooled from one side of the cassette to the other.

After a minute the tape came to a shuddering halt, and the button snapped back into place.

Putting the machine back on the table, he walked toward the little kitchen. He opened a cupboard door and took out a half-drunk bottle of scotch he'd brought with him, Ed poured himself a large measure.

"I think I'm going to need this." He said to himself as he prepared to listen to the tape.

He sat back down at the table and placed the glass next to the tape recorder. His index finger wavered over the play button.

Picking up the glass he took a gulp. Placing the glass back down, he resolutely presses play, and the tape begins to roll.

The first fifteen minutes were nothing but the static hiss of the tape recording its own motion. He was just starting to feel a bit of an idiot to think there might be something to this, when he hears what sounds like a distant voice.

He leans into the recorder, turning the volume up.

Amongst the hiss, there it is again. Yes, it is definitely a voice. Then another. Muffled but clearly a voice. They are getting louder and louder, he can start to make out the odd word.

The hackles on the back of his neck are standing up. A conversation is coming into earshot. One, two… three, four… five men, talking, talking about songs.

Oh, my god, was this the band?

Then came raised voices, an argument?

He hears one storm out, another goes to get him. More discussion. Then, other voices, strange accented voices, that seem to come from a different place. There comes a loud crash from the tape. It makes Ed jump, he reaches toward the machine and is just about to turn it off when a very clear voice says;

"Halo Eideard, thasinn air a bhith a' feitheamhriut." <Hello Edward we have been waiting for you>

Ed drops his glass. The voice is coming from beside him. Turning, there are two men standing beside him. They are bearded and dressed in garb from another time.

Ed blanches in terror, but before he can say anything, one of them raises a large heavy club and brings it down sharply on Ed's head.

"Bidhsinn ag ithegu math a-nochd." <We will eat well tonight> they say as they drag his limp body away into the shadows.

Via Dolorosa

"Wake up," Immanuel's sister puts a hand on his shoulder. She gives him a shake, "Immanuel, wake up."

Immanuel stirs. He slips his hand under his glasses and pinches at his nose. He pushes them to the top of his head and rubs his eyes.

The hard plastic chair he's been sitting on for the last week is uncomfortable, and has hurt his back. He blinks a few times and sits up straight. Returning his glasses to his face, he looks at his sister.

"She's gone."

His sister holds out her hand.

Immanuel takes it and stands. They both stand in silence for a moment.

"When did she go? I've been here all week. I was just shutting my eyes for an hour. They said she was comfortable."

"She was, Immanuel. They said that sometimes people wait to be alone before they pass. It's quite common."

"But I'd promised her I'd be there until the end."

"You were. No one could have done more."

Immanuel feels his head. The headache he's been nursing for the last week suddenly intensifies. He jams a knuckle into his temple.

"Do you want to see her for the last time?"

He nods.

Immanuel pushes open the door to the side ward where his mother's body lies. He stands at the foot of the bed. His mother looks much younger now the pain has gone. Her furrowed brow and wrinkles have fallen away, she seems almost serene.

She looks better in death than she did when she was alive," he says to no one.

Walking to the side of the bed, he takes her hand. It is cold and stiff.

"Goodbye mother." He plants a child's kiss on her forehead, arranges the blankets about her, turns and leaves the room.

Ten days later, his sister is getting a drink for an elderly relative they haven't seen in years.

There are a lot of people, they haven't seen in a long while, who have turned up for her funeral.

Immanuel and his sister are hosting the wake at the local pub their mother hated.

"I'm sorry about your mum," another relative says.

"Are you?" Immanuel snaps back. "Are you? Are any of you? When's the last time you bothered with her? She's been ill for years. Not a single one of you came to visit. Not one..."

"Immanuel." His sister comes over to him and puts her arm around him. She ushers him out of the room and into a corridor.

Immanuel leans against the wall and crushes a knuckle into the side of his head.

"Have you stopped taking your medication? You know how this goes once you stop taking it."

"I don't need it anymore. I only took it because mum made me, and now she's gone. I don't need it."

"Immanuel, you do need it. Do you remember how you were before the medication? You weren't well. Remember the hospital? Remember how many times you were in the hospital?"

Immanuel did remember, but he had it all worked out this time.

"I won't go back there."

"No, you won't, if you take your medicine; now where is it?"

"In my drawer."

"Right, when this is over, we're going home, and you're taking it."

Immanuel looks at his sister and nods.

He knows he'll never take it again.

He hates the way it makes him feel: muzzy, like he is standing behind a net curtain. When he was on the medication, it flattened life out, stacking moments like a pack of unshuffled playing cards.

He only feels present when he is free of drugs.

His brain thickens and begins to tightly fill the inside of his skull. He grips the back of his neck. He just needs to get through this afternoon, and then everyone will leave and he can get back to normal.

His sister guides him back to the wake. People are leaving now. They have all heard about Immanuel's 'condition'. After his outburst they don't want to be around to witness what comes next. Besides, he is right about his mother. No one had come to see her in life, mainly because she was a cruel and sadistic woman.

Her sharp tongue and quick temper were enough to keep most people at bay. They also felt Immanuel's strangeness, and it made them feel uncomfortable.

His sister is the only one of his family most people like. She is the very definition of forbearance, yet she had had the good sense to get away while she was still young enough to have an independent life of her own.

Her occasional forays to see her brother and mother were swift, by design. She had persevered for years, taking the children with her so they could see their grandmother and uncle.

She stopped putting the children through the ordeal, after the old woman was so needlessly vile to her daughter, over the way she ate a sandwich, of all things, that she made her cry for the whole journey home. Following the incidentshe vowed never to take them again.

Immanuel sits on an uncomfortable plastic chair in the back room of the pub. He feels the base of his spine. It's not much better than it had been ten days ago.

He looks at the half eaten beige platters; he's not eaten a thing, and isn't going to.

The last person to leave the wake is saying goodbye to his sister; she leaves the room with them.

Momentarily, Immanuel sits alone. He can hear the sounds of the bar next door. There's another entrance just behind him that leads into the public bar. A figure bursts through it.

"Alright Manny?"

It is his brother.

"Not in the nuthouse yet then? I thought they'd have you in there like a shot after the old girl karked it. Or have you got a weekend pass?"

Immanuel grits his teeth at the sound of his brother's tobacco voice. Being older than him, his brother knows how to get under his skin. The pain in his head surges at his arrival.

"What are you doing here?"

"My mum too, Manky. I thought I'd see if the old bag had left anything for me. I'm staying with you tonight. Is that ok?"

It isn't.

'Manky,' the juvenile taunt the fat slob always calls him. The prick.

His sister reappears.

"Fuck me, the toxic halfpenny has finally turned up. I thought you might make an appearance. Come for the money, have you?"

"That's a nice way to greet your big brother. I can see time hasn't mellowed you any, Sis. You sound more like the old bag every day."

"There's nothing for you here, so why don't you fuck off back to the cesspit you crawled out of."

Immanuel puts his hands to his ears. He squeezes as hard as he can. Their noise still manages to penetrate his skull.

"Look, you're upsetting Immanuel."

"How the fuck can you tell? He's a nut job." He approaches Immanuel. "You're a fucking nut job, ain't you, Manky?"

He grabs Immanuel's wrist and starts yanking at it. "Can you hear me? Nut job Manky. Can you hear me?" He lets go and falls backward. Stumbling, he catches himself on the bar.

"Just go, will you?"

"Not until they've read the will. When is it?"

"It's tomorrow, but I'd be amazed if there was anything for you. All you've ever done is take from Mum, especially since Dad died. You only brought misery and pain to her door, not to mention nearly bankrupting the family. If there's anything left, I doubt you'll see any of it."

"That's where you're wrong, dear sister. You know I was always mum's favourite. First born and all that bollocks. She was falling over herself to give me money. She knew there was no point in giving it to Dr. Doolally. He'd give it away to the people living in his head. Still hearing the voices, eh, Manky?"

He sneers and drunkenly laughs as he slaps his hand on the bar. "Barkeep! Let's have some drinks."

Immanuel stands and faces the appalling man.

His brother is in his mid-fifties, his face unshaven, hair unkempt. The suit he's wearing is stained and smells faintly of urine and spilt beer. He brings his hand down on the bar again.

"Barkeep!"

Immanuel turns to leave.

"Don't worry Manky, I'll be along later, once I've seen the old bag off properly…"

Immanuel stiffens again. His sister throws an arm around him and leads him to her car.

A short drive later, they pull up outside the family home.

"Immanuel, I want you to promise me that you'll take your medicine. It's what Mum would have wanted. She hated to see you the way you get when you're not taking it. Remember what she said?"

Immanuel did remember. If she suspected him of not taking his medicine, she would get the riding crop she kept from her youth, and whip him with it until he'd taken all of his pills.

He could feel the strokes as keenly as if she were still striking him now.

"Will he take the house?"

"I don't know. Mum never could see him for what he is. I hope not, Manny. Let's worry about that after they've read the will."

"Look, Immanuel, I have to go. The children are with a neighbour, and I need to get back. It's at least an hour and a half's drive from here at this time of day, and I really need to get going. I'll be back tomorrow morning. Don't let that bastard brother of ours into the house."

He promises he won't, and that he will take his medicine, and waves his sister goodbye.

He watches as her little car disappears around the corner. Immanuel feels for his door key, unlocks the front door, and stands in the hallway.

It is so quiet.

Toward the end, his mother had been bedridden, and hadn't made any noise at all to speak of, but it is still quieter without her in the house.

He suddenly feels very tired. The headache is getting worse again. Maybe his pills will help.

He goes upstairs, and on his way to his bedroom; he passes the half-open door to his mother's room. He hesitates on the threshold.

Immanuel takes a few steps back and finds himself in his room. Involuntarily, his hand goes to his head again. The pressure is getting worse.

Opening his bedside drawer, he looks at his medication. Four boxes of brightly coloured pills. He reaches in and picks up a packet.

As he does so, he thinks he hears something just behind him. It sounds like someone clearing their throat. Then comes a whisper.

"Don't."

"Don't?" He repeats. "Don't what?"

He goes to the window and looks at the house on the other side of the street. A middle-aged woman lives there. Some nights, he sees her through the window. She'd look up and wave at him. She would mouth words silently at him.

They had a secret language. Sometimes she would say, "How are you today?" Sometimes she would tell him of things that were yet to happen, and sometimes she would try to warn him.

She is there now. She has a young man with her, she often has young men with her.

She looks up at the window and waves.

"Who's that?" says the young man.

"That's my crazy neighbour. He gets locked up every now and then. It pays to be nice to him, I don't want him murdering me in my bed now, do I?" She laughs, and the young man laughs too.

Immanuel can clearly see the message she is trying to send him. He watches their conversation carefully. She mouths the word 'murder'.

She's trying to warn him. His head throbs again.

Murder. He sees it, clear as day: murder.

He turns back to the bedside cabinet, replaces the pills, and snaps the drawer shut.

Immanuel walks downstairs and into the kitchen. He takes the largest knife from the block and goes to the sitting room. He makes his way to the chair by the window, it's his mother's chair. He sits in it and looks out onto the street.

He holds the knife in his left hand.

The serrated blade catches the light as he fidgets in his seat.

He puts the radio on. They're playing something classical; he doesn't know what. The music ends.

Immanuel waits for instructions. The announcer speaks, "Immanuel, Immanuel, are you listening?"

"Yes. I'm listening. What am I to do? I'm told there is murder about, what should I do?"

"Be prepared, Immanuel."

"I am. I have a knife."

"Good, Immanuel, good. They are here, they are in disguise. They could be anyone. You need to be prepared, Immanuel."

Immanuel's headache rises. The pressure is building and building. His vision starts to fade. Starbursts of shimmering light jump before him. He feels as if his eyes might fall from his skull at any minute.

"Be prepared, Immanuel." The voice fades, and the music resumes.

Immanuel closes his eyes for a moment and tries to catch his breath.

He's brought back to the room by the sound of breaking glass coming from down the corridor. It is the sound of the kitchen door being smashed open.

"Be prepared, Immanuel," the warning rolls around the room.

From the direction of the kitchen, coughing and swearing fills the air.

"Be prepared, Immanuel."

He is prepared. He tightens his grip on the knife.

Immanuel gets up from the chair and stands behind the living room door. What is making that noise? It doesn't sound human.

From the other end of the corridor, a hellish, blasphemous fiend crashes through the back door.

The creature is rank and emits stale, pungent fumes that catch in Immanuel's throat.

Murder. His neighbour had warned him. The beast is in the house. It's going to kill him.

"Be prepared, Immanuel. Be prepared to do whatever you have to. It's you or it, Immanuel."

"Yes. I see it. It's me or it. It's here,"

His head is swirling. The creature stumbles into the front room, snorting and snarling. The spittle-flecked lump falls to the floor. It's back arches as it tries to get back on its feet.

"Fucking hell, what the fuck do you think you're doing, Manky you little prick. Why isn't the back door open?"

"It knows your name, Immanuel, kill it. Kill it now. Kill it before it kills you!"

Immanuel raises his hand and brings the knife down on the back of the monster's neck with as much force as he can muster. He slashes at the hunched figure. Stabbing with the serrated blade. Slashing and cutting.

"Make sure, Immanuel. Make sure."

"That's it," his mother joins in, "Kill it, kill it!"

He stabs again and again and again, until all the strength has gone from him. He slumps down over the prone creature.

Silently, a pool of blood seeps out from underneath the carcass, making Immanuel's clothes sticky and wet.

He takes his glasses off and is about to wipe his eyes when he sees the blood on his hands. He is holding a knife. It too is covered in blood. He drops it.

Immanuel gets to his feet. He looks at the slumped figure in front of him and the rapidly increasing puddle of blood that's soaking into the living room carpet. His mother will be furious with him. She loves that carpet.

"I can't let her see the carpet like that."

Immanuel decides to wrap the body in the rug. He'll put it in the old privy, it's just outside the back door. She never goes in there anymore, so it will be safe until he can clean up the mess.

Crunching through broken glass, he drags the cadaver down the corridor and with effort, wrestles the bundle into the outhouse.

He looks back down the hall at the long red sticky smear.

"Mother mustn't see this." He opens the kitchen cupboard, gets the mop and bucket out, and starts to clean. It takes him quite a bit longer than he's expecting, but he manages to mop it all up.

It is now very late. The radio has fallen silent. He listens to the static. There are no further messages today. He turns it off and goes upstairs.

Pulling his mother's bedroom door to, he calls,

"Goodnight mother."

Going to his own room, he lies down on the bed. His head feels a little better now, so he shuts his eyes and falls asleep.

There's barely a pause before it's morning again; he wakes with a start as someone hammers on the front door. Immanuel feels for his glasses on the bedside table. Putting them on, he goes to the window and pulls the curtain to one side. It's his sister.

He looks at his watch. 10am. The woman over the road comes to her gate and calls to his sister. She turns, waves, and joins her on the other side of the street.

He can see them. The neighbour keeps looking up at his window. She's trying to tell him something. He can't make out what it is, so he turns on the bedside radio for an update. He twiddles the dial until the static dissolves and the familiar voice starts to speak.

"What are they doing, Immanuel? They're talking about you. You know they are."

He looks through the window again. Are they crying?

"Crying?" He says, feeling his head; it's starting to ache again. The heaviness is building. So much tension.

"Why are they crying, Immanuel?"

"I don't know."

The women go inside the neighbour's house and pull the front door shut.

"They're up to something, Immanuel. Be prepared."

His head is filling up. He can hear the blood squeezing through his veins, pounding in his ears. It throbs to the rhythm of the radio.

"Your head is so very full Immanuel. Does it hurt? I bet it hurts. So much pressure. I can help you Immanuel."

"How can you help me?"

"Go to the shed Immanuel."

He clutches his head with both hands and turns from the window. Immanuel makes his way down stairs and through the corridor. The broken window in the kitchen lets in gusts of morning air. Reaching the shed, he goes in.

"Now Immanuel. Take the drill."

Immanuel moves to his workbench and picks up the drill.

"Now go back to the house. To the bathroom."

Dutifully, Immanuel heads upstairs, drill in hand.

"Put the drill down, Immanuel. I want you to get a biro from the drawer by your bed."

He puts the drill on top of the cistern and goes to his room. Opening his bedside drawer, he pushes his medication to one side, and fumbles for a pen. Finding it, he makes his way back to the bathroom.

"Where does it hurt, Immanuel?"

He points to a spot above his left eye.

"Mark it with the pen, Immanuel."

Standing in front of the mirror, he takes the pen and draws a blue dot on his forehead, just above his left eye.

"Now, Immanuel, do you want to release the pressure? Think how good it would feel. Let all that pressure out. You wouldn't need the drugs then, would you?"

He shakes his head.

"Pick up the drill, Immanuel."

He hesitates.

"Pick it up, Immanuel," his mother tells him. "There's a good boy."

Immanuel picks the drill up and places the tip of the bit on the blue dot on his forehead.

"I want you to turn it on. You must release the pressure."

He squeezes the trigger. The drill starts to spin. The pain is almost unbearable; he relaxes his grip.

"What's the matter with you, you stupid boy? Do you want to get better, or would you prefer to go back to the funny farm?"

The voice taunts him; the radio joins in.

"He's scared, he won't do it."

"He's always been useless."

"I'm not scared!" He shouts as he tightly grips the handle of the drill and presses it hard into his scalp.

The noise and vibration as it grinds its way through his skull is almost unbearable. His teeth bounce off each other and his vision dissolves, but he presses on.

At least it's stopped hurting now that he's well into his skull as the stench of burning bone fills the bathroom.

The drill is starting to run out of battery as the tip of the bit breaks through the remaining few millimetres of matter and touches his brain.

An involuntary spasm in his right arm almost shoots the drill across the room; he falls to the floor.

From downstairs, the banging on the front door resumes. There is an urgent, muffled discussion from the other side, and the voices quickly fade.

A minute later, they are at the back door.

"What the fuck has gone on here?" His sister asks the neighbour. They both look in horror at the river of blood that's coming from the outhouse.

His sister reaches for the latch, lifts it, and the door swings open. An arm falls from a gap in the carpet, and the blood-spattered face of her brother blankly stares out at them.

"Oh my god. What's he done…"

His sister steadies herself and looks to the house.

"I'm calling the police."

The neighbour gets her phone out and dials 999.

His sister takes a breath and gingerly enters the property.

"Immanuel, Immanuel, are you there?"

She can hear footsteps on the stairs.

"Yes, yes, I'm here."

"Immanuel, what happened? Are you ok?"

"I've never felt better, dear sister."

She moves down the corridor toward him.

Immanuel stands at the foot of the stairs, with his back to her.

"What have you got in your hand? Is that a drill? Immanuel, what has been going on?"

"Nothing to worry about, sister; I was prepared."

Immanuel turns toward her. Blood pours from the drill hole in his forehead.

Barely able to believe her eyes, she backs away from him and makes for the door. Gripped by terror, she's unable to make a sound as she falls backwards into the garden.

Immanuel is feeling fine.

He can see a jet of steam escaping from the hole in his head. Bright lights dance in front of his eyes, and a chorus of voices call and sing his name. The pressure is relieved.

"Nothing to worry about. I was prepared, and now I'm better."

He stretches his arms wide and holds the drill aloft in triumph, as the distant sirens grow louder.

Four Minutes

"Where is everyone?

Hello, hello, who is it? Who is this? Your number isn't recognised. You're garbled. Who is this?

Judith?"

THE NUMBER YOU HAVE DIALLED IS NO LONGER IN SERVICE

"Judith?

Fuck sake the horizon's on fire

The horizon's on fire

Judith."

The Hexham Heads

Part I

"Come on, we'll never get there at this rate. It's already twenty past eleven, you haven't got your things in the car yet. Mullion is a six-and-a-half-hour drive on a good day. I don't want to miss the dinner I've already paid for!"

Clara picks up her walking stick and manoeuvres her leg around the kitchen table. Steadying herself on the cane, she winces as she rises and sets off for the front door.

"I'll wait in the car." Picking up her handbag, Clara puts the strap over her head and adjusts it so as not to hamper her walking. Grimacing slightly, she takes a few steps forward. Muttering under her breath, she surfs along the furniture, making her way toward the car on the drive.

Vicky, stands in the bathroom, and leans on the sink. In one hand is the lipstick she's reapplying. "I won't be long mum." Pulling a tissue from the box, she blots it on her lips. She gathers up her mascara and eyeliner, and places the cosmetics back in the overstuffed bag, that comprises the mobile section of her extensive makeup collection.

Scooping up her handbag, she walks downstairs.

Scanning the hall, she does a final check to see whether all the luggage has made it into the car.

Noting that it has, she closes and locks the front door, and walks up the gravel drive to the carefully packed red Honda. Vicky opens the driver's door and settles herself into the seat. She reaches behind her and places her handbag on the back seat.

Clara stares ahead. She takes a handkerchief from her sleeve and blows her nose.

"Right. Shall we go?"

"YES!"

Vicky starts the car and pulls out of the drive. She turns right and heads in the general direction of Cornwall.

Once upon a time, Clara would have balanced an oversized map of wherever they happened to be heading on her knee for the entire journey.

She would point out places of interest along the way, and recount stories of trips she had taken with her late husband and the trouble they'd got into.

However, the advent of the ubiquitous satnav meant that she no longer needed to provide this function.

Instead, Vicky's phone barked out instructions at regular intervals in a shrill and needlessly posh voice. This left Clara free to make helpful driving suggestions approximately every two miles along the way.

Precisely six hours and thirty two minutes later, they arrived on the Lizard peninsular.

Mullion is about seven miles outside Helston. Although it's a small town, its size increases exponentially during the tourist season and it gets very busy indeed. Too busy really, which is why Clara and Vicky choose to visit in the depths of winter.

December is a bitter month in Cornwall. The wind off the Atlantic is bracing to say the least, and every type of weather rolls in around every two hours.

The only thing that remains constant at that time of year is the biting wind, which will cut you in half if you're not ready for it.

They pull up outside the tiny Spar in the middle of town. Vicky takes a breath. "Aside from gin, is there anything else you want mum?"

Clara thinks for a moment. "Yes, some oatcakes if they have any."

"Mum, there's some in the back. Do you want me to get them for you?"

"No! They are for the room. We might need some for the car."

Vicky counters, "Ok, fine, I'll look for some but I don't think I'm going to find any in there. I mean look at it."

They both crane their necks to see the inside of the shop. It's tiny and pretty much the last place you'd expect to find oatcakes.

Unbuckling her belt, Vicky opens the car door and gets out. She gives a small stretch and reaches for her back.

That was a long drive and her back hasn't been brilliant for quite a while. They've already had to cancel this trip once, as the last time they were due to go she'd found herself incapacitated. The slipped disc rendering her immobile and in pain for five weeks.

Still, they were here now, so she'd see what she could find inside the shop.

Ten minutes later and back in the car, she proffers a cheese straw toward Clara from a box she's already started.

"What's that?"

"A box of cheese straws. It's all they had. Well, aside from the gin. Do you want one?"

"Completely, indigestible!" Clara looks at the pastry with utter disdain.

Vicky begins to take them away, only for Clara to snatch the pack from her. Hurriedly removing one, she starts to eat it.

Wearily, Vicky gets back in the car and adjusts the mirror. Starting the engine, they pull out onto the road.

About two miles on is the holiday cottage they've rented. It's a standard sized Cornish fisherman's cottage, which means it's small. They pull up outside and sit looking at it.

"Gosh, it's tiny."

"We did know that when we booked it, it's actually a lot smaller than I realised, but what a view!"

Across the road from the cottage is the cliff edge. High cliffs run off to the left and the Atlantic Ocean is battering them with a poetic fury.

It's quite at odds with the sudden burst of sunshine that accompanies their arrival.

Seabirds wheel about in the simmering air, occasionally dropping from view, as they fish the rough waters below.

"Well, this is worth the drive isn't it Mum? Breathe some of that air in. Nothing between us and Newfoundland." Vicky takes a deep breath and looks out to sea.

Clara opens the car door and the wind takes hold of it and rips it from her hand.

"Wait there Mum, I'll help you."

Clara recently had her eighty sixth birthday, and despite the not so long ago hip operation, she is showing no signs of slowing up. If anything, it's given her a renewed lease of life. She's not going to win any egg and spoon races, but she is mobile once more, and free from pain.

Vicky comes to the side of the vehicle and helps her to her feet. Stick in hand, Clara holds onto the car and looks out over the stunning Cornish cliffs.

"Wow. How beautiful."

They both pause for a second.

Just then the sun disappears behind a cloud, and a few spots of rain begin to fall.

"Shall we go in?"

Vicky nods, opens the front door to the tiny property and manoeuvres her mother inside.

Since her step dad died, Vicky has taken it upon herself to take her mum on holiday at least once a year. This has gone on for over twenty years now; when Clara was a bit more mobile, they had undertaken road trips all over the UK and Europe.

In the car they would get, and off they would pop.

Some of the trips had been more successful than others. However, they had always found them entertaining and they took great delight in regaling the stories to everyone else upon their return.

Now Clara was so much older, these trips tended to be shorter in distance and duration, although Cornwall had been somewhere they had both wanted to return to; having spent many happy days there when Clara's husband was still alive.

This might be the last occasion they attempted something quite as adventurous, as it was a lot of effort for both of them. Vicky was heading toward sixty herself and aside from her back issues, she found these trips to be quite taxing.

Usually, they followed a pattern. The first morning was filled with anxiety and quite a bit of friction between them both. Inevitably, they would fight for most of the journey.

Clara would goad Vicky about her driving or the amount of luggage she had brought with her. "It's three fucking days!"

A lot of the journey would take place in icy silence, only punctuated by the passing of 'digestible' snacks between them.

Inevitably the snacks would turn out to be completely indigestible.

Shortly, a voluminous and loud dyspepsia would follow. Vast columns of noisy air would be expelled by both of them at two-minute intervals. This could last for up to an hour at a time.

If they'd have had the foresight, they would have invested in a methane powered car, and driven the two hundred and twenty-five miles to Cornwall for free.

Once they arrive at the destination, more fractious behaviour would ensue while the bags are decanted and rooms taken up. There would follow a period of relative calm, while they'd both get their breath back, and begin settling into their temporary home.

From this moment on, peace and harmony mostly reign. They both have their roles whilst away, and once they rediscover them, there is no need to scrap any longer.

The next morning, after the fitful sleep one has when away from your own bed, they awake and have the first breakfast of the day.

Leftover sandwiches from the journey, the cheese straws and two dissected apples that would keep them going until they could ablute and dress.

Outside, the weather is doing its usual thing. Icy blasts of horizontal rain, then bright blinding sunshine, which would be immediately followed by more rain and wind.

Even though cliffside walks have been discussed, there is more likelihood of being scraped from the path by the coruscating wind and deposited over the edge, than actually enjoying the view.

Between them they decide that today will be a good day to go for a drive and see what they can see.

Once dressed, and in the car, a map appears from Clara's handbag.

"What's that for, we can find our way around with the satnav".

"Yes, I know, but this is more fun. This map has lots of interesting things on it and I like map reading. You don't mind, do you?"

Vicky, looks at her little old mum in the seat next to her. She seems so old and frail these days. Vicky casts her mind back to the time when Clara was mother lion, bringing up three children alone. All those years, ploughing on, working all the hours she could to keep everything going.

Vicky recalls how after a long day at work, Clara would come home to their tiny bungalow. Once the evening routine was complete, she would sit, cigarette in hand, looking out of the window, waiting for everyone to go to bed, so she could sleep on the couch, the only available space left to her.

"No mum, of course I don't mind," and with that they set off.

Whilst chatting, Vicky had been driving somewhat aimlessly, for about twenty minutes.

"Where are we heading mum? We're going to drop off Land's End in a minute"

"No we're not. We're heading in exactly the opposite direction. I think."

Clara lifts her glasses onto her forehead and squints at the map.

"Vicky throws her a look.

"Yes, turn here!" She jabs a finger toward the right turn they are about to sail past.

Vicky brakes hard and just makes the turning.

"Bloody hell!" shouts Clara.

"A bit more warning next time would be nice mum."

The turning quickly narrows down to barely a single track.

"What the fuck have you brought us down here for? There's not even a passing place. I'm not reversing up this road if something comes!"

"It didn't look this narrow on the map." Clara squints harder at the faded cartography. The 'road' has dwindled from a thin line to the faintest of marks on the ancient chart. It might even just be a hair that's got stuck on it. Clara brushes her hand over it and it disappears. She says nothing.

"How much further is it?"

"Just keep going, I'm sure we'll be out the other side soon."

Vicky brakes. "What do you mean? Give me that map."

There's a short struggle before Vicky wrests it from Clara's grasp.

"Where are we?" Vicky scans the faded contours.

Clara leans over and waves her hand vaguely over an area of green. "Here somewhere."

Vicky sighs. "So we're lost. Brilliant. Mum, why didn't you just say so?" She reaches for her phone and opens her satnav app. There's the familiar icon of the car but it's sitting in a sea of white, featureless nothing. "Fan-fucking-tastic. No signal"

"We might as well go on then," Clara offers.

They have little choice but to proceed, Vicky accelerates cautiously as they head further off the beaten track.

After around fifteen minutes of bouncing around on unmade roads, they turn a corner, and to their mutual delight, see what appears to be a shack about five hundred metres ahead of them.

"Finally! Somewhere to turn around."

As they near it, they can see that it's not just a shack, but also appears to be some kind of gift shop.

"Who would put a gift shop here? It's literally in the middle of nowhere, down a non-existent road!"

Vicky pulls the car into a pot-holed gravel car park and turns the engine off. They both sit there, staring ahead.

There's a flip sign on the front door of the gift shop, and it emphatically states that it is 'Open'.

"We might as well have a look now we're here," Clara suggests.

"We might as well. They might even tell us where we are." Clara ignores this and they both get out of the car and head toward the shack.

The shop is no more than a large ramshackle garden shed, with a rusting corrugated iron roof. Its only concession to being a shop is the large picture window, which sits in a gently rotting wooden frame.

Vicky pushes at the door, lightly at first, then realising it's going to take a bit more force to budge it, she gives it a proper shove. The door flies open and Vicky almost tumbles over. Gathering herself she looks behind her, Clara is already making her way in.

The shop is tiny, it's made even smaller by the sheer number of objects lining the walls, ceiling and what little floor space there is. In one corner there is a small counter with a side door directly behind it.

"Bloody hell, this place is small," Clara says. She leans on her stick and peruses the many 'gifts' available to buy. She pokes at a few items with her stick.

"Careful Mum, I don't want to have to pay for any of this tut if it gets broken."

It is at this point that the side door snaps open, and the figure of a very old Cornishman appears in the doorway.

If there was a picture of a stereotypical Cornishman in an encyclopaedia, this gentleman would be it.

He's wearing loose fitting corduroy trousers, a blue fisherman's smock and a patterned neckerchief. On his head sits a blue fisherman's cap.

"Can I help you?"

"We're just looking thanks."

"Mind as all you are." He gives a small chuckle and winks at Clara.

Clara perks up at this.

"Not many gets down here. What you looking for?"

"I was just showing my daughter some of the more obscure parts of Cornwall."

Vicky stifles a "Ha!"

"Then you've come to the right place!" He laughs and Clara and the shop owner are away. They natter on in the background.

Vicky has tuned out now, and is working her way through the cluttered shelves, looking for a souvenir for their holiday. After a while, right at the back of one of the shelves she spots two small carved stone heads.

She reaches in and pulls them out. They are not quite like anything she has seen before. About the size of a tennis ball, each has a roughly carved and heavily weathered surface. The impression of a strange looking face is scraped into each one. Vicky turns them over in her hands, examining each one closely.

She doesn't like them, but is fascinated by their course appeal. To her own surprise, she calls to the shopkeeper, "How much for these?"

The shopkeeper abruptly stops talking to Clara, and lets out a muffled sigh, "Bloody hell, not again," he mutters under his breath. He edges around the counter, passing Clara and gently takes the stones from Vicky's hand.

"Sorry. Not for sale."

"Why are they on display then? How much do you want for them? £20? 25?

"Not for sale lady."

"Alright, £40 the pair."

"No sorry lady. They ain't for sale. I'm closing now, if you'd like to make your way out."

"50 then."

"I said NO! Now please leave."

He bundles them out the front door, slamming it shut behind them. Flipping the emphatic sign to CLOSED, he wrenches down the blind and turns the light off.

""What did you want to go and do that for? He was just telling me about his daughter, she works in Penzance. What did you want with those revolting stones anyway, and fifty pounds! Have you lost your mind?"

Vicky reaches the car and puts a hand on it. "I-I don't know. I just felt drawn to them. It was the strangest thing. I felt compelled to own them. I don't even like them. But, but I felt, and don't think I'm nuts, but I felt like they wanted me to take them."

"I always said you had an imagination on you. You should have been a writer. Ha!"

Vicky recovers her composure, they turn the car around and with the light failing, head back the way they came, and on to the cottage.

The rest of the holiday passes quite quickly, and before they know it, Vicky is waving goodbye to her mum, before setting off for the run-down seaside town she calls home.

••••••

Part II

Vicky drags her bags back to her apartment. She lives on the ground floor of her block, so getting the bags back in isn't too difficult. Dumping them in a pile by the door, she goes to the kitchen to make herself a warm drink.

Vicky looks at her phone. It's been a long drive and a long day, and she's absolutely done in. Yawning a couple of times, she gets undressed, pulls on her thin cotton nightie and gets into bed. For once she isn't plagued by incessant indigestion and falls into a deep sleep.

Abruptly, at 6:30am her alarm goes off. She's half way into the shower before she remembers that she is still on holiday, and has no work for the next week.

Relieved, she returns to bed and attempts to get back to sleep. Vicky does briefly drop off, but is woken suddenly by the sound of a loud thump. Startled, she lifts her head and looks at the clock. It's nine thirty. Her head falls back onto the pillow. Although woken by the noise, she quickly forgets it.

Finding her phone she checks for messages. There's one from her mum. She'll read it later.

Vicky takes the half empty mug of leftover drink and gets out of bed. Shuffling and yawning she makes for the kitchen. She barely washes the mug before refilling it with hot chalky water and an organic tea bag, which immediately splits in the cup, leaving grouts floating in the brew. She groans.

Vicky returns to her bedroom, puts the grouty tea on a mat on her bedside table and bends down, pulling her suitcase toward her. Lifting it from the floor and onto her bed, she lazily unzips it, and flips the lid back. It takes her a couple of goes as it seems determined to stay closed. Getting mildly annoyed with it, her left hand opens it fully and presses the flap into position.

She takes a sip of her brew, fishing out the larger leaves as she goes. Vicky starts to unpack the bag. Lifting out the evening frock she didn't wear, she spots something wrapped in newspaper at the bottom of the case. She clears the area around the object and reaches for her glasses from the bedside table.

Picking up the carefully wrapped parcel, she feels the weight of it in her hand. It is surprisingly heavy.

Furrowing her brow, she wonders aloud, "How did these get here?"

Placing the package on her knee she carefully peels the wrapping from the parcel. It is wrapped in yellowing newspaper, The Falmouth Packet. She tries to read the headline but the ink has faded and she can't make it out. There are more layers of brown paper underneath, which she quickly removes.

Drawing back the final layer, her mouth falls open in astonishment at what she sees.

There in her hands are the stones she had tried to buy from the shopkeeper in Cornwall.

"How the fuck did they get there? Mum must have gone and got them. But how?"

Confused, she tries to work out how she could have bought them and put them in her bag?

Clearing up the paper, she places the heads on her bedside table and arranges them so the 'faces' are staring straight at her.

Reaching for her phone, she calls her mum.

"Mum, this is going to sound weird, but do you remember that gift shack we found when we got lost?"

"Of course I do. I may be old, but I haven't lost my marbles just yet."

"You didn't go back and buy those stones I was looking at did you?"

"Of course I fucking didn't. Why would I? They were revolting".

"Ok, thanks. I thought I'd just check."

"Are you ok. You sound odd."

"No, no I'm fine. I'll call you later. Love you," and with that, she hangs up.

"That's very weird. If mum didn't buy them, how did they get here?"

Examining them closely, she can see that each stone has a distinctly different 'face'.

They are worn but there are enough of the features remaining to make out the anguished expressions on each one.

Vicky is a bit shaken by their sudden appearance in her luggage, but not as freaked out as she might have expected to be. The impression she got in the shop was that they wanted to be with her.

Removing them from the bedside table she gets up goes to the hall. Once there she puts the stones on the shelf, that lies either side of the front door.

None of this was making sense. Somewhat unnerved, she goes to the bathroom and runs herself a bath.

When the bath is half full, she takes off her nightie and gets in. The water is warm and feels good. Lathering her hair, she slips below the surface and begins the process of rinsing and conditioning her curly locks.

From under the water, she hears the unmistakable sound of heavy footfall coming from inside her flat.

Surfacing quickly, she wipes the suds and water from her eyes only to see what looks like the back of a dark figure hastily exiting her bathroom. She jumps and almost inhales a great gulp of bath water.

"What the actual fuck was that?" She sits up and reaches for the towel beside her. She gets out, covers herself, and stands there dripping.

She's not sure what to do at this point. Her phone is still in the bedroom and she can't make it to the front door without going in the same direction as the shadow she thought she saw.

"Don't be ridiculous Vicky. It's the middle of the morning, no one is going to break in in the middle of the morning. Get a grip of yourself and go and have a look".

Gingerly she pokes her head around the bathroom door. Still clutching at her towel, she edges into the living room, passes the kitchen, and makes it into her bedroom.

There is no one there, her flat is empty. She checks the doors and windows. All locked tightly shut. Still damp, she struggles into her clothes.

A shiver shoots through her. "I just need to go for a walk, get some fresh air, that's all I need."

She quickly dries her hair, pulls on her hat and coat, and sets off for the beach.

Several hours later she returns. It's a windy day and despite the hat, her hair is quite wild now it's been blown about so much.

She takes off her coat and sits at her dressing table. Picking up the hairbrush she begins to run it through the tangles, working at the knots and snags.

Vicky automatically closes her eyes whilst she does this, as she always has, when she hears another odd noise.

Not loud this time, more of a snuffle. Like something sniffing the air. She abruptly stops brushing and opens her eyes. Putting down the brush she looks about her.

Nothing.

Getting up from the table she looks through the doorway into the next room. Her gaze is drawn to the stones on the shelf. Have they moved?

She moves toward them. Why yes, they have a little.

"That must have happened when I shut the front door." She reasons. Straightening them once more she opens and shuts the door a few times. They don't move a millimetre.

"But it must have been that", she says to herself.

Although she tries to ignore it, she can't quite fully convince herself of this, so taking the stones from the shelf, she opens the back door on to the courtyard garden.

"I'll just leave these out here for now," she thinks. Shutting the door behind her, she feels a little relief that at least they are not still in the flat.

A year passes; the incident in the bathroom fades from her immediate recollection. Vicky is getting ready for the Christmas holidays. Her friend Colleen has come to stay.

"Park yourself in the spare room, and I'll make some tea."

"Got anything a bit stronger? It's been a long journey and I'm desperate for a ciggie, where should I go?"

Vicky pops her head round the door, "Wine ok?"

"You bet, red if you've got it, please."

"No problem, the smoking area is through the living room and out the double doors. Make sure they're shut behind you. It's freezing out there. We've even had snow forecast for this evening."

Colleen picks up her fags and lighter and drags her woolly hat over her hair. Pulling her cardy tightly around her, she opens the doors and steps into the courtyard.

Finding a seat, she perches on the edge and speed smokes her way through a tailor made. It really is getting cold.

Stubbing out the cigarette, she notices the two stones sitting on the retaining wall of the flower bed. She gets up and goes over to take a closer look at them.

Picking up first one, then the other, she examines them closely. Despite the cold they feel quite warm to the touch. "Odd?" she thinks to herself. She sets them down and heads back into the flat.

"Where did you get those stone carvings from?"

"Ha, that's a good question, I'd almost forgotten about them. When I was in Cornwall with mum last year, I came across them in this odd little shop at the end of a very rough single-track road."

"I tried to buy them but the shopkeeper wouldn't sell them to me, in fact he threw me out of the shop! The curious thing was, when I got home, they were carefully wrapped in newspaper sitting in the bottom of my bag. I don't know how they got there."

"What? Don't you think that's a bit strange?"

"Yes of course I do, but what am I going to do about it? I can't post them back; I checked on Maps but there's no sign of the shop. There's no one to ask, other than Mum, and she swears blind it was nothing to do with her.

They did creep me out a bit, so I put them in the garden and basically forgot about them."

"Well, that would do more than creep me out, I can tell you. Do you know what they look like?"

"Some poorly carved faces?"

"Well, there's that, but they also look like the Hexham Heads."

"You what?"

Colleen is a lecturer in history at Northumbria University; so Vicky's ears prick up at this information.

"The Hexham Heads; they look like them, not that I've ever seen them, no one has, well not for forty years.

The Uni had them for a while. They ended up in the British Museum after that, then they disappeared and they haven't been seen since."

"Are they worth anything?" Vicky jokes.

"Dunno, probably. It's not the value they're infamous for…"

"Infamous?" Vicky didn't like the sound of that.

"No, it's the story that comes with them that's the kicker. Have you had any strange events happen to you while they've been here?"

"Why? Yes. I have actually, that's why they're out there. I thought I kept seeing things moving about in the flat."

"Things?"

"Well, shapes, dark shapes, a couple of times, but nothing since they've been out there."

"That ties in with the story."

"Do I want to hear this?"

"I don't know, do you?"

"Well, you've started now. What's going on in my head can't be worse, so you might as well get on with it."

"Ok, what about that wine?"

Vicky pushes a large glass of red into Colleen's hand.

"The Hexham Heads were discovered by two children in the early seventies, they dug them up in their back garden, in Northumberland. The family didn't think much of them and used them as door stops. However, after a short while, there began a series of sightings."

"Sightings? What do you mean by sightings?"

"Brace yourself coz this is the spooky bit. There were sightings of a large half human half wolf like creature that was said to stalk neighbouring houses apparently looking for something. It was seen several times by several different people, and upset the family and the boys so much that they offered them to a historian in Southampton they knew. She bought them and added them to her collection."

"Not long after, she started seeing things too. One night she came down to find a large wolf-like creature standing at the foot of the stairs. It vaulted the railing and ran into her kitchen. She was terrified, but felt compelled to follow. When she got to the kitchen, it was gone."

Vicky was looking quite anxious at this point, but Colleen continued

"It happened a couple more times, until she decided that she didn't want them in her house anymore; she gave them to the British Museum. They were on display for a while, but the staff started complaining about seeing things, disturbing things.

It got to the point where the unions got involved. None of their members would work in the part of the museum where the heads were, so they were removed from display and put into storage. When there was a stocktake a few years later, they discovered they were missing. No trace has been found of them ever since."

"And you think my stones are these heads?"

"They look like them."

Colleen taps at her phone and pulls up a pencil sketch of the stones and pings it over to Vicky's phone. She opens the message and pinches and zooms around the rough drawing.

"Why are there no photos?"

"Dunno. You'd think there would be some, but I can't find any. The pencil sketch is all we've got."

They do look like 'my' stones.

Vicky opens the patio doors and retrieves them from the yard.

She sets them on the table and holds her phone up beside them.

"Oh crap. They really do look like them. I'm going to take some photos."

She takes about a dozen photos from all angles.

"What am I going to do with them now?"

"They might be worth something, they've been missing for quite a while and there are people who'll pay very good money for these."

"I can take them for you. I know a few collectors. They're always buzzing around the history department, trying to get opinions on things they've unearthed. You shouldn't have any trouble shifting them"

Vicky gladly hands them over to Colleen.

Colleen picks some socks out of her case and carefully drops one stone in each of them. She wraps more clothes around them and packs them away.

"Thank you Colleen. I'll be glad to see the back of them to be honest. I've never liked them. They make me feel uncomfortable, and after what you've just told me, I really don't want them here. You're ok to take them? Aren't you bothered by the stories?"

"I'm going to take them straight to the Uni. We've got a vault I can put them in. They'll be alright in there."

They both head into the kitchen, and between them, make and eat a meal. Following a long catch up over several glasses of wine, they decide it's bed time and retire to their respective bedrooms.

Around 2am, Vicky stirs. Advancing age has meant that she now must go for a piss at least once a night. She lies there, hoping the sensation will fade away, except it doesn't. Bowing to the inevitable, Vicky slides out of her warm bed and into the freezing air of her bedroom. Pulling the curtain aside, she looks out onto the street.

The snow has really come down in the last few hours, and it's laying quite thickly on the ground. She holds herself to try to keep warm and heads for the bathroom.

Only, she doesn't get that far.

From Colleen's room she hears snuffling and scratching. She cocks her head to see if she can identify the noise. She can't. Advancing toward the door, which is slightly a jar, she can hear something moving in the room beyond.

"Colleen," she calls softly. "Colleen," a little louder. She has one hand on the door and gently pushes it open. She is not prepared for what she is about to see.

Standing at the foot of Colleen's bed is a very large dark figure. It has what look like very muscular human legs, but the top half isn't human. It has the head and torso of a huge black wolf, and stands over Colleen. Vicky can see its breath in the cold air, snorting and snarling, looming over the sleeping woman.

Vicky stifles a cry and claps her hand to her mouth.

It hears her.

The creature turns toward her, she can now see its hideous face staring straight at her.

A long snout sniffs the air. She tries not to move, but it's no use. The bladder full she's been holding onto starts to trickle down her leg. The creature sniffs harder. It can smell the urine as it puddles on the floor.

With one swift movement the beast leaps from the bed and lands just in front of Vicky. It draws itself up to its full height, it must stand nearly seven feet tall, its pointed ears brush her high ceiling as its head tilts toward her.

Colleen stirs, which momentarily distracts the monster.

Vicky gathers herself and tries to run from the room, she slips in the puddle and falls to all fours, scrambling to get away.

Rediscovering her voice she starts to yell "Colleen. Colleen." Running, as if through treacle, she makes for the bathroom, slamming the door shut behind her.

Silence.

She's breathing hard and leaning on the bathroom door.

From outside the room, she can hear soft footfall, and then a gentle knock.

"Vicky? What's the matter? There's water all over the bedroom floor."

"Colleen is that you? Is it really you?"

"Yes, it's really me. What's going on?"

Vicky gingerly opens the door a crack, still bracing herself against it. She scans the hallway. Colleen is standing there alone in her night things.

"There's nothing there with you?"

"No, of course not. Are you ok?"

Vicky opens the bathroom door. Her night dress is soaking and she's obviously terrified.

"Christ! Look at the state of you. What's the matter? Did you have a bad dream? Shit, let's get you cleaned up."

Colleen takes Vicky in hand and gets her in the shower. She rummages in her cupboard and finds another night dress. All the while Vicky recounts the events she has just witnessed.

"Vicky, I wish I'd never told you about the bloody Heads now. It's just a wild story. You were having a nightmare. Look, there's nothing here." Vicky dries herself and puts on the nightie Colleen has found for her.

Hand in hand, they both go round the flat together and double check. No monsters there. Colleen cleans the floor up and they go to Vicky's bedroom.

"Don't leave me alone," Vicky pleads, so they both get into her double bed and attempt to see the night out. Sometime around 5am they manage to drift off to sleep.

It is the late morning when Colleen's phone wakes them up. Her father has been taken ill, and she'll have to go that afternoon.

"I'm sorry about your dad, and this might not seem appropriate, but will you still take the stones with you? Please?" Vicky implores.

"Yes, they're in my bag, see?" She shows her the socks where she's stored the stones.

"Thank god. Are you sure you're ok taking them, that story, and last night has made it so I don't even want them in the garden now. Please take them away. I don't want anything more to do with them."

"I'll take them ok. Try not to think too much about them. You had a bad dream, they happen. I blame myself for getting you rattled in the first place."

Colleen packs up her things, and Vicky drives her to the station. They embrace; Colleen turns and waves as she makes her way toward her train.

"Hope your dad's OK. Keep me posted," she calls after her.

Vicky feels a little silly now. It probably was a dream, and Colleen's father being unwell was more real and pressing than her ridiculous overactive imagination.

Two days later, it's Christmas Eve. Vicky has put the incident with Colleen out of her head, or tried to, and is instead concentrating on her last-minute Christmas shopping.

Snow is still coming down: it has transformed the dreary streets into a slippery wonderland. Some of the steeper hills have some grit on them, and she is fortunate hers is one of them.

Arriving at her door, struggling with her shopping, she tries to find her key. At that moment, her phone rings.

"Not now mum," she says to herself. Her phone is actually to hand so she pulls it out and looks at who is calling her. It's Colleen.

"Oh no. I hope it's not about her dad."

Locating her key, she lets herself into her flat and abandons the parcels in the hall, the phone is still ringing, she answers it.

"Hi Colleen, it's not your dad is it?"

"Hi, no, no, he's getting better thanks; that's not why I'm calling you…"

"What?"

"I don't want to alarm you, but I can't find the stones."

"What? What do you mean?"

"The stones. They weren't in my bag when I got home. I was going to call you earlier but what with the business with dad, I didn't get a chance. Are they still at yours?"

"What? No, they're not here."

She quickly scans the room. "No, not here."

"That's fucking strange. Well, forget I said anything. I don't want to give you another nightmare."

Vicky gives a nervous laugh.

"Are you ok? You don't sound right."

"No, I'm fine, just as long as they aren't here, I'm fine. I'm off to mum's tomorrow for a couple of days, so I've only got tonight here on my own."

"Ok, I'm sure they must be here somewhere. I'll take another look. We both saw them in my bag, didn't we?"

"Yes, yes, we did. I hope your dad keeps improving, send him my love and happy Christmas."

"Yes, you too. Send my love to your mum. We must meet up again soon. No bad dreams this time eh?"

Colleen hangs up; Vicky has a good look around her flat, just in case. No, the stones definitely aren't there.

She feels relieved, and starts to run a bath. After a long soak, she gets out and dries herself. She reaches for her nightie and pulls it over her head.

As she pulls the garment past her eyes, she is met with the sight of the two heads on the shelf directly in front of her.

She freezes.

"How the fuck…"

She reaches out and picks them up. Examining them, she realises they are indeed the stones.

An icy blast of fear hits her. Then, from somewhere behind her she can hear heavy breathing, a stench fills the air. A stench of rotting things.

In the bathroom mirror she catches sight of a beast. A huge beast with ravening jaws. It's standing just behind her and is poised to jump.

Its clawed hands flex, reach forward, grasping for her.

Her breath catches in her throat. She is so terrified, all she can think of is escape. Still clutching the stones, she runs from the bathroom, through the flat and out into the bitter night air.

Wearing only her nightie, she runs through the freezing streets. She can hear the monster behind her, it's getting closer and closer. She can feel its breath on her neck as she slips on the snow and ice. Her bare feet provide little traction. She is screaming hysterically as she tries to escape.

The beast begins to bear down on her as she reaches the bridge that spans the gorge, that separates the old town from the new.

She runs to the middle and stops. The beast is within touching distance now.

She turns to face it. Holding the stones aloft, Vicky shouts at the monster in front of her, "Is this what you want? Well, go and get them then. "She tosses the stones over the bridge and into the waters below.

The monster bares its teeth as if laughing. It raises a finger and wags it slowly from side to side, shaking its head as it does so. Then, it very deliberately points at her.

All the air leaves her body as the realisation of what is about to happen dawns on her. The beast takes a step forward and pulls her toward it. It's cold dead eyes bore into her as it lifts her from the ground.

A snarl plays about its thin lips. Vicky can feel herself being overwhelmed by the beast. The monster gently puts her down and begins to meld with her body.

Shortly, only Vicky is visible on the bridge.

In a last act of human defiance, Vicky steps over the railing, and is about to throw herself from the bridge and into the roiling water below, when from behind her she hears a voice.

"Hey there, are you ok?"

Don't forget the there's an audio version of
these stories read by Saul Reichlin, Alex
Lowe, Eva Pope, BC Camplight and more.

Scan the QR code below or go to

https://tinyurl.com/4h4hs22u